The Jersey Shore

Also by

WILLIAM MAYNE

RAVENSGILL

THE INCLINE

A GAME OF DARK

EARTHFASTS

ROYAL HARRY

THE BATTLEFIELD

and many other titles

WILLIAM MAYNE

The Jersey Shore

HAMISH HAMILTON
LONDON

First published in Great Britain 1973
by Hamish Hamilton Children's Books Ltd.
90 Great Russell Street, London WC1B 3PT

SBN 241 02238 X

Printed in Great Britain by
Western Printing Services Ltd, Bristol

For BIDDY

I

THE JOURNEY lasted all night and all day. Even before the night had closed against the windows of the train Arthur had seen for long enough the ample horizons of America running along the edge of the sky. When the daylight deepened into blue twilight and then swooped into blackness he was glad to be able to stop looking from the window at a view that never became anything.

The morning landscape was the same. Arthur himself felt he had been slept in, the train felt as if it had been slept in, and the country outside seemed to have stood still all night. His mother did not know how the land went, when he asked how much longer the train would be making its way through the rising green corn. 'Nobody," she said, "told me geography this far east."

Perhaps no one had told the land what it ought to do this far east. Some time there had to be a change to sea; the sea was where they were going. Everything had looked the same for so long that the train might just be going round in some large circle, like a model. Arthur thought that cars and wagons on the roads, as they showed themselves and were hidden again, might be toys; that the trees standing here and there might be manufactured; that the crops were cut from green cloth; the houses from card.

The sea should soon come. He watched the gentle distance outside, wondering whether some far shading on it might be the beginnings of water, whether a grey patch of actual lake or pond or the thread of a creek might suddenly become a bay or an inlet or an estuary. But the water would not come and flow over the land.

About mid-day he lost all expectation of it. Hills began to appear, like clouds banked on some shore, giving him a first hope that travel was nearly done. The cloudiness turned to solid earth, and then to rock and slope and forest. The train went up a valley, twisted under a heeling sky, its windows closed against a chill in the air, and stopped at a new kind of perched town, clamped to the rocks of the mountains, with roads gripping the spaces between the houses like claws.

The train waited here long enough for them to get out and buy a meal next to the station. Then they stood in the sunshine but out of the mountain wind, breathing the new light air until the train was ready to leave again.

Now it went downhill for four hours. Some of them were very long hours indeed because a mist had fallen on this side of the mountains and there was nothing to be seen and the coach was cold in spite of the summer. In the last hour of the four the mist gave way to a long endless rain, dropping on an empty land, hanging and dripping from close pine trees, hanging low over broad muddy rivers, and then at last polishing the roofs of a town.

The town began with scatters of houses, near the line and far from it. Then another pair of rails joined the set Arthur's train was using, coming in over a bridge and fastening in with a click and a jerk that set the coach swaying. After that the houses crowded close and low, gradually crushing out of existence all trees and fields. It was a watery city under the downpour, at first under the natural light of the sky and then, when that had been smoked out, under the glitter of electricity.

The train began to sink into the city. The houses grew taller, until they were no longer houses but buildings and then not mere buildings but skyscrapers, not equal with the coach any more but bigger than it. The train crawled among the roots of the structures, like a snake among branchless tree stumps, and then it burrowed underground, taking shelter, and came to rest in a dark, hot, clammy cave.

The train was to go no further. Arthur and his mother got off, and waited for the crowd to clear before asking for directions. Then a conductor who was too used to telling people the way sent them to another part of the station, where the next train would be. Before going to wait for it they went for something to eat.

"I wish this was over," said Mother. "This chair's on the solid ground, I believe, but to me it buckets around worse than the train did. I can manage fine on the train, but being on land again just makes my stomach uneasy."

She leaned back against the wall and closed her eyes. She went to sleep for quite a long time. Arthur wondered whether to wake her, in case they missed the train. He knew the time now, because there was a perfectly good clock on the wall of the restaurant, but he did not know the time of the train. He decided that his mother would know when to wake, because she knew the time of the train.

She woke with a sigh after nearly half an hour. "We'll go," she said. "You should have waked me, Arthur." She drank her cold coffee, made a face at it, picked up the case and the basket, and led the way out. Arthur picked up the wicker box and the cloth bag and followed her.

The platform they had to wait on, underground again, was filling with rich people, he thought. They had black shining shoes and blue suits and very settled hats and they were not wrinkled like the people at home. They carried neat leather bags and umbrellas. They looked at Arthur and Mother, and their luggage that was just as it had come from home. Arthur felt that there was a difference between the beginning of the journey and this middle part of it. When they began they had been smart travellers, taking with them the sorts of things they would need. Now, somehow, they looked as if they had begun travelling a hundred years ago, before people really knew how to do it. They were old-fashioned, different, shabby.

Mother had thought the same thing. "City folk," she said. "They aren't real; they couldn't manage where we come from. I'm whispering because I don't dare say it out loud among 'em here."

"I guess not," said Arthur. "You act quiet when it's Indians all around." So they made themselves a stockade with their travelling goods, the rubbed case, the basket, the wicker box and the cloth bag, and stood inside their circle, safe from the disregarding but treacherous strangers.

When the train came, they thought the journey was over. These same strangers moved suddenly and dangerously, picked up the old case, the basket, the box and the bag and began to take them away. But as soon as the attack began Mother knew what it was. These city folk were not robbing them but helping them on to the train, putting their goods up and finding seats for them, and then leaving them alone.

"I think we've been taken hostage," said Mother. "It doesn't hurt so far."

"These are Mexican Indians," said Arthur. "They live underground."

The underground did not last long. The new train began to move out of the cavern and into the tunnel. Then it came out in a groove between the tall buildings, and climbed to the surface of the city, and the rain washed everything in sight, bright on roof and dark on walls, black on the street and silver in the gutters.

There were short stops at lonely platforms. The city workers got off the train and it grew emptier and emptier.

"When do we get down?" said Arthur. "Do you know?"

"We'll jump off when I get my hands untied," said Mother, still being an Indian, though Arthur had stopped.

"Sure," he said. "But do you know when?"

"It's the last stop but one," she said. Arthur thought that was a good definition, until he realized that you can't know when the next stop will be the last. But when he looked up to ask whether she really knew she spoke before him. "It's called Arnott's Bay," she said. "And your Aunt Deborah will be there to meet us."

Something tore a hole in a cloud and a spout of sunshine came down, and was eaten up by the falling rain. The gap did not close, but grew larger, and soon there was a body of sunshine floating in the atmosphere, some way off to the side of the railway track. The sunshine became warm enough to burn its way to the ground, where it began to lift up a stringy mist. There grew more of it and more, and then the cloud and rain had gone and there was a white-blue sky and a disc of sun, almost with a black line round it where it had been drawn.

At the next halt a new sort of air came into the coach.

"The Atlantic Ocean," said Mother. "Do you smell it, Arthur?"

"Nearly a smell," said Arthur. It was not quite a thing he could name, not quite a flavour. It was partly a feeling, like steam in the nostrils, perhaps, or like being punched on the nose and the moment before the feeling of being hurt comes real.

"You should be able to get it better than me," said Mother. "From what your father says, your grandfather was never out of sight of the Atlantic all his life; he couldn't live without the salt in his lungs."

"That was in England," said Arthur. "A long time ago."

"Not so very long," said Mother. "But you'll be able to ask him before the day's out."

"I forgot," said Arthur. He had never seen his grandfather, his father's father, the English one, who lived no longer beside the English seas but on this New Jersey coast. Arthur expected it was with his Aunt Deborah, his father's sister.

"There isn't a grandmother," he said, not quite making it a question.

"No," said Mother. "None left on that side of the family."

"None?" said Arthur. "Were there several?"

"Three, I think," said Mother. "Or four. All English but one."

"All at once?" said Arthur.

"It's different in England," said Mother, and Arthur was not sure how serious she was. "One at a time," she said.

The train was now in sunshine all the time, coming in warm. The track was lifted above the surrounding countryside on an embankment. To one side they saw into the middle of trees with occasional clearings where stubby bushes grew. To the other side were long level fields and a dull grey distance, where it seemed the clouds had not cleared.

"That's the Atlantic," said Mother.

Arthur looked, and could find nothing to name. He began to realize that the expanse was not some ugly remainder of weather but the thing they had come to stay beside for several weeks. That dull grey distance was what they had come to. It was nothing like the long plain they had travelled through since the night before. That had been very much the same all over, after a time, because it had been made of the same objects repeated time after time: little clumps of trees, broad endless fields with some few sorts of crops, clusters of houses, a net of roads all sliced by the railway line, a water-tower, an artesian well, a generator tower, once even an airfield full of biplanes. That day-long sameness had at least been made of different things, and the sea should have been capable of the same differences, with rocks, islands, whales, mermaids, ships, water-spouts, and particularly a proper blue colour and curling waves with white crests. But there was only a tepid grey, without brilliance or twinkle or life, as far as his eye could see.

"It's just like that today," said Mother.

"It's like a desert," said Arthur.

"It must be different, sometimes," said Mother. "Icebergs in winter, perhaps."

Arthur reminded her that they had come for the summer. But they came among the buildings of Arnott's Bay and to a stop that had a faded name written once on it, so gone away with time that if the sun had not been on it they would never have read it.

There was one woman on the platform, and she was not

eager to greet anyone. She waited until they had got themselves out of the train and stood beside the wheels before coming forward.

"Miriam," she said. "This will be Arthur. He's not very big for his age. That'll be the English side of the family. My pa never was a tall man."

Arthur thought it would be strange if he had never been a short man, because people grow but don't shrink. But he knew that Aunt Deborah was not quite the sort of person to say that to, any more than his father, who was her brother, was. Mother was the one to get behind remarks to the ridiculous things people were really saying.

"Come along home," said Aunt Deborah. "You'll want to freshen up after that trip."

"I won't hurry about anything, Deborah," said Mother. "I have to get my land legs a minute, or I'll throw up right on the tracks."

"Some days she just does," said Arthur. "Coming out from town in the truck."

"Things keep on moving," said Mother. But the worst moving thing went away then. The train pulled out and went on to its next and last stop. "It was mostly that going past my eyes," she said. "Turning me."

Arthur could tell that Aunt Deborah had not liked being called by her first name, Deborah, by Mother. He thought she was not used to it at all; no one knew her well enough to call her by her name. He thought he would try to avoid calling her Aunt Deborah. Aunt would be enough.

Mother was ready to walk now. Aunt Deborah picked up the cloth bag from the heap of luggage, and carried it. Arthur hoisted up the wicker box, and Mother took her usual load.

14

They crossed over the track and walked down the bank and into a sandy lane. The sunshine struck up hot from the sand. No rain had fallen here today; there was no dampness at all in the top two inches of the sand. They walked quietly, only the tumbling grains underfoot talked of their going, only the creaking of the wicker box mentioned anything.

Aunt Deborah heard it make its noise. "Is it a cat?" she said.

"It's a python," said Mother, but when she saw the rage and horror on Aunt Deborah's face she quickly said it was a joke and that there was nothing in the box but clothes. Aunt Deborah thought the joke was just as repulsive as the python. They walked on in silence again.

The house was wooden, and stood more upright than a house need. They went in, and stood by the varnished walls, in a complete silence.

"I'll draw a pitcher of water and you can wash all that travel off you. I don't think there's much the boy can harm, Miriam: I put away the tender things."

II

TWILIGHT HAD COME, and the darkness following, and the unbelievable stillness of the garden beyond the window had changed to an impossible calm black. Arthur found himself expecting, at each second, that the house would start moving, like the train. Once he thought it had begun to move, but the noise and the trembling of the floor and walls had been caused by the train they had left, returning along the line again and passing a hundred feet away on its embankment.

When he went to bed he did not sleep at first, because every time he relaxed he started awake again, missing the shake and rumble of the railway. He had dropped off at last, on his benchy mattress with the cold hard sheets lying under and over him and not surrounding him closely like the sheets at home. Then Mother had come to bed herself, and lit the room with a candle. He looked at the wooden wall with his shadow on it growing out of the grain. Mother pulled back her bedspread and got into bed, slowly. Arthur turned over and looked at her.

"Hard beds," she said. Arthur rested his elbow on his mattress and his chin on his hand. The mattress echoed like wood.

"There isn't a grandfather," he said. "I've counted all the rooms, and there isn't one he could be in."

"She hasn't mentioned him," said Mother. "But she hasn't said much yet about anything. There'll be a piece of house we haven't seen yet. We'll find out about it in the morning. And perhaps he didn't want to be troubled with us at the end of the day, being an old man. He can't be far away, your own grandfather and Aunt Deborah's father."

Arthur looked at the candle burning between the beds, the flame still like a flower on its stem now that no one was moving in the room. He felt the moving of the train in him again, tipping him suddenly forwards so that his head fell off his hand and his arm dropped lifeless on to the mattress and everything was dark. He wondered why it was so, and found that his eyes had closed in sleep. He opened them again but they would not stay open and see Mother and the room. She said something to him but he could not hear it. He slept.

He dream-travelled all night, and all the dry land of the day was changed to water; blue trees of sea, lagoons of fields, hedges and divisions between crops standing as waves ready to break, huge tides of mountains sucking back from the water-girt coach he voyaged in and then coming in a plunge forward and sweeping past on either side and below and drily above. His pilot, or captain or driver (because he did not know which sort of vehicle he was in) was an old man, in charge of the water as well as guiding the train or ship or the moving land.

When he woke all was still and peaceful. Mother still slept. Light came round the curtains at the windows and framed with reflected gold from the varnished wall the black square of thick cloth. He sat up, got from his bed and pulled a curtain back.

There was no bright expected sunshine, but only a still mist, not very thick and not very moist, hanging in the yard of the house. There was no sound in the house or out of it. No one was yet moving. He went back to bed and slept again on the hard bottom sheet.

He woke again because there was a dog scratching under the bed. It was only a dog until he was fully awake, and then he knew the noise was outside, a passing train heaving its morning way along the coast through Arnott's Bay. Mother was awake now.

"I don't know what time we ought to get up," she said. "I don't want to be underfoot at the wrong time of day. She might take a broom to us and sweep us to one side as if we were cats, geting us out of the way. If we stay quiet we'll hear her moving about."

"Are you scared to get up?" said Arthur.

"That's it." said Mother. "It might be the wrong thing. We'd better start right; we're going to be here several weeks. She used to be a jolly girl, playing the guitar and talking until all hours. But that was when your father was courting me, a long time ago."

"I expect no one came for her," said Arthur. "It makes people go dry and fussy. I've noticed it."

"How have you noticed that?" said Mother.

"It happens every day at school," said Arthur. "All those girls that don't get a date just act as if they didn't care, but you can tell they do care, and then they act kind of mean, but some girls no one would want for a date, like Maureen Taski, well, just think."

"She's quite a nice little girl," said Mother. "Pretty, too."

"Creepy," said Arthur. He could not explain why Maureen was creepy; it was just a thing that the whole school under-stood. He tried not to think of her. He thought of Lorna

Rackham instead. "I have to write to her every day," he said. "That's what she told me; but I guess it won't matter until next week."

"She'll forget you," said Mother.

"Sure to," said Arthur. "If she doesn't forget me no one else will date her and she'll turn into a creep and I won't want to know her when I get back. But what I want to know is, is Aunt Deborah a creep grown old?"

"That's not a kind question," said Mother. "She's your aunt, not mine, so you've to find the best side of her. She'll have one, she just hasn't had time to show it yet. And remember, you've got a best side too, and you haven't had time to show it to her, either. That's two of you on trial, and you both have to win."

Aunt Deborah tapped at the door then and said there was hot water waiting. Mother got up first and washed, and sent Arthur along next. While he waited he looked from the window. Aunt Deborah moved about in the yard outside, among things growing there, in her apron, coming in and out of sunshine now that the mist had gone. She was putting up a washing line.

When they had both washed and dressed they had breakfast. They were made to feel uncomfortable during the meal because Aunt Deborah did not sit down to it with them but stood outside with the wash tub doing her laundry, soaping and rinsing and twisting dry and then laying the garments in a basket and covering them over. Every few minutes she had to stop and attend to her guests, who did not like to eat much or often because they were putting her to trouble.

The train went by once again. Aunt Deborah poured Mother more coffee and went out into the garden with the washing.

"We should have got up sooner," said Mother. "It's nearly nine. She must have been up for hours, lighting the stove and toiling over the wash, and here we are in her way."

"She isn't cross," said Arthur. "She just doesn't talk much."

"I'll wash the dishes," said Mother. "But I'll ask first."

Aunt Deborah came in, dried her hands thoroughly, and sat at the table. "It's a matter of fitting things in," she said. "I have to get that line of clothes in before noon, or the next train through will smoke them black. Now I'll have my breakfast, but I didn't like to ask you to wait, Miriam; you'll be used to early breakfast with Clifford working and Arthur at school. Here there's just me, and I please myself."

"Just you, Aunt Deborah?" said Arthur. "I thought I had a grandpa round some place."

"Oh, Pa," said Aunt Deborah, as if she were talking about a gate or a mailman or some one that meant something to her but not much. "He lives down the road a piece."

"Not here?" said Arthur.

"We wouldn't like that," said Aunt Deborah. "We've got no great liking between us. But you go and see him any time, boy. He has ten minutes' talk in him these days, and that's all; then he repeats himself. He's getting old, it's true, but he still manages."

"Arthur's been looking forward to meeting his grandfather," said Mother. "Clifford and I haven't seen him in twenty years."

"Nothing changes in him," said Aunt Deborah, "except he says the same things a bit sooner now, a bit more often."

Then she started to have a large breakfast. She was so used to having it alone that she took no more notice of Arthur and Mother. They left the table, almost without being noticed, and went to their room and made the beds and pulled back the curtains.

"I wonder if I *should* open the window," said Mother. "Some folk don't like it because of the flies and there aren't any screens up." In the end they did open the windows, because sleeping in a room makes it stuffy. Then they went into the garden at the front of the house and the yard at the back and looked about them.

There was the sandy railway embankment all along one side, so there was nothing to be seen in that direction, just the bank, the road they had come along, and the fence. Behind the house westwards there was a reedy marsh with yellow flowers growing but no living water. To the north there lay a grassy field with a couple of trees edging in the view beyond it. Southwards there was a sort of sandy desert with the railway to one side, and the road winding across it, more a mark than a way. Down the road there were one or two low buildings.

"It'll be one of those," said Arthur. "Do you remember, Mother?"

"Your grandfather?" said Mother. "I don't recollect much about him, Arthur. I thought he lived in this house here, but now I look at it I don't see how he could have. I never slept here before last night. When I came to visit your father before we were married I stayed up in the village and just visited here a little, and I never rightly got to see how little the house was. He was here one or two times, I know, but he never took notice of us, I think. If he lives down in one of those places there I can't tell you which one. Aunt Deborah will know."

Aunt Deborah, when she had finished breakfast, said she did not have time to take Arthur down the road. She said she would point out which house it was. But when she came to show him which one she found herself in a difficulty.

"Well," she said, "I know it so well I don't think I've looked for years; why should I look when I know what it's like? But now I recollect that I never could see much beyond the garden fence, my eyes are so short-sighted. But I did see clearly one time, and I'm just about sure I had some spectacles, in a gold frame." She screwed her eyes up and gazed as far as she could, but there was nothing there for her to see but a golden haze. "Now I recall that I haven't seen a train go by this long time. I thought maybe I hadn't looked, but maybe I just didn't see. If I can't see, you'll have to see for me. What is there out there."

Arthur looked out across the sand. He saw three distant buildings and several trees and a fence and probably goats. But he said: "It's just crawling with Comanches out there."

Aunt Deborah took no notice. She went on looking south-wards.

"There are three houses, way off," said Arthur, quietly and soberly.

"I think it's the middle one," said Aunt Deborah. "I used to live in it when I was a girl, and it was the middle one when we walked up from the other side, but like as not it won't be the middle one from this side. If I could just see the roof I'd know, by the angle of it. No, you'll have to guess, Arthur. You'll know him. He's English."

Arthur found he could go at any time but had to be in for meals. He had a pocket watch and it had travelled with him, too deep in the pocket to be useful. Now he went indoors and got it and let it down into his shirt pocket and buttoned the flap over it. Then he skipped over the fence, out of Aunt Deborah's range of vision.

The garden in front of the house had been shady. The sunshine had not long been beating down on it because the railway shaded it first thing. The road moved away from the railway bank and into the desert. Here it was hot and still for a time. Then the wind climbed the bank and dropped on the road, bringing a steamy heat with it. One step Arthur had been dry, the next step his shirt clung to him and the heavy air pressed his shoulders. His lips felt dry yet moist as well. He licked them and his skin tasted of salt. It had been brought on the wind and settled on him.

He walked on, more slowly. He began to see what Aunt Deborah meant by not being sure which house was the middle one. Looking ahead he saw two of them seem to melt together when the road curved round a marshy place. When it came back to its old line the houses moved apart. Then the road angled away from its line and the houses moved in relation to Arthur and he no longer knew where each one had been at the beginning. That did not matter, of course, since Aunt Deborah had not been able to point any of them out exactly, but it was still confusing because when he had found out which house was the right one he would still be muddled when he got back to Aunt Deborah's, and Mother might never be able to learn which was which.

In the end he came on all three houses at once, when the road wound its way to a point central to them all. They were all equal. They were all silent as well; or if there was a little sound coming from any of them it was carried off by the wind. The wind was stronger now, but still clammy, still sticky with the sun's heat.

Out in the desert a goat called. There was not really a very large desert. Arthur could see all its edges. The straight edge was the railway bank, and the other edge was all one, like part of a circle, rising up towards fields and trees. It was as if the railway had cut straight across a piece of beach and left it waterless.

He went to one of the houses. It was a ruin. He could see right through it, where the boards had fallen away. No one lived in it. He went to the next. The walls were solid. There was a stoop, with a chair on it. Beside the chair there was a lumpy rug. Arthur walked up on to the stoop, meaning to tap at the open door to the room beyond. But the rug got up and bit him, just one bite that did not let go. It was not very painful; in fact it tickled more than anything. He thought that things were not appearing as they should. The first time he had thought of dog that day it had been a train. Now that he thought of rug it was dog. He tried to move his leg away from the dog's teeth, but it growled and shook its head, trying to worry him. It tickled so much he laughed. The dog let go, sat down, and growled at him.

An old man came out of the room and looked at him. "Set down, lad," he said. "I'll tell you of your father's brethren that he never knew; and of my daughters that were; and of all of both that never were. Set you down."

III

"THERE NOW, what had he to say? Pa, I mean," said Aunt Deborah. Arthur had come into the yard just by the time he had been told to, and she was there handing down undergarments and aprons and table-covers from the drying line. She had looked at him for some time without speaking. She was used to living alone, without talking, making up for herself what other people intended.

Arthur thought in his turn. After the dog had bitten him and then fallen off his leg with exhaustion, there had been those words from the old man about his father's brethren. Arthur had sat on the stoop, half in the sun and half out of it and the ruggy dog had laid itself near him, on the shady side, and breathed heavily and smelt of dog.

The old man had gone in and out of the house a number of times, and talked at intervals, about one thing and another. At one moment he would step down to the ground outside and wait and listen for someone. At another he would sit on the chair and say things that Arthur knew well enough already.

"Nancy was the last of them," was one of the things he said, and it was hardly a new thing to Arthur, though it sounded like one, because the old man added "Deborah" so that Arthur understood that Nancy was another name for Deborah. He knew Aunt Deborah was younger than his father, Clifford.

"I was a lad like you," he said at another time, and Arthur was again not surprised. "An English lad," the old man added, looking closer at Arthur. Arthur thought that that was the biggest difference between him and the old man when young—one was English and the other American.

"I had three wives, turn and turn about," he said at another moment, when he had been indoors and filled a pipe with tobacco, lit it with a wooden match, and come to sit on his chair again, with blue smoke about him. That Arthur knew as well.

Arthur moved himself until he was against the house wall and leaning on the sand-worn wood, golden in its grain, with all its strands and knots and sinews lifted for show, worked at by the weather and the sand flung on it by the seasons of the year, all the soft parts taken away. The wood wall was warm in the sun. The old man was warm in the sun, smoking with his eyes closed, worn by the sand and the seasons in the same way as the wood, to a like colour and texture.

Not many more words had been exchanged. The old man had had a letter from Clifford. Arthur said very little. He felt he had no information that could be useful to his grandfather, and he had been asked no questions. He had looked at his watch now and then, and at twenty to twelve, when the watch was the only speaking thing in the whole world, he had got up to go. The dog had stretched out its head and opened its mouth. Arthur saw the teeth smooth and blunt, worn down by the same sand that had worn man and house, and then the mouth closed, not having succeeded in engulfing anything.

"I'll go now," said Arthur.

"I'll be here, times," said the old man. "I'll tell you yet."

Arthur had left him, stepping out into the hot sand that had worn itself into a powder. Heat came up from it. Heat shone back from his grandfather's house, from the derelict house he had to pass near. He looked back at the third house. Someone lived there. In its yard, sitting on a bench, was an enormous black man, with the white collar of a priest. The priest lifted one shirt-sleeved arm, called out in a low, powerful rolling tone, "Bo-oy," as a greeting, and waved his thumb towards the old man's house. Arthur understood this to mean: "Is that your grandfather?" and gave a similar signal back.

He had left them to their different solitudes.

Aunt Deborah had taken down all her washing. Arthur went forward to carry the basket for her. "Well," she said, "he didn't say just nothing, did he?"

"No, I guess not," said Arthur. "We had quite a talk." He was glad that that satisfied her. There had not been many words in the visit, but words are not everything. He thought that he and his grandfather understood each other, without words. There were things waiting to be told between them that would need more than speech, that would need long times of sitting on the stoop against the wall, and waiting for the thoughts to join his mind.

"Well, that's fine," said Aunt Deborah.

"And dandy," said Arthur. Aunt Deborah took no notice of this unserious remark.

A day went by, and then another. Arthur learned the trains and could tell the time by them. They came at mealtimes, he found, and at getting up time. He found out that the man who had waved to him from the other house down the road was called The Preacher, and that his house was his church. On Sunday he saw people going down to worship there, and later he looked down and saw them, too many to fit into the building, singing hymns on the open sand; he heard their harmonies coming along the wind, without being able to distinguish the melodies.

One day he and Mother walked out on to the beach somewhere the other side of the railway, and looked at the sea. For part of their walk it was grey and for the rest it came up a greened blue, more as it should have done if it had been transformed from a field. It went down the sand as they passed, and came up again as they came back. Out on it there were islands now, and in it passed ships of a small sort and barges. None of them called at the town of Arnott's Bay.

He went down to his grandfather's house again. Nothing was different. The dog looked at him with an opal eye. The old man blew amethyst smoke.

"Time I was a lad," said the old man, "on a east coast like this back at Osney, against the sea."

"Atlantic," said Arthur.

"No," said the old man, telling him something new. "It was the German Sea, and yonder is Holland, that's Low Germany, and the English Holland is north, on our side the sea. The German Sea. There's the wall against it, like so," and he pointed a dribbled pipe at the railway embankment that cut across the view. Arthur understood that somehow the sea could be higher than the land, that the land was only borrowed, and that England was being talked about, not New Jersey.

"Osney," said the old man. "Osney there was, and Osney Cold Fen, and Osney Battle, all places, and a church to each, and I've lived in two of them. A church to each. And not like . . ." He left the words on the air, on the smoke of his pipe. Arthur knew what he meant, what the churches were like, or not like. They were not like the third building out here, not wooden huts.

"A parson to each," the old man said. "To each a priest. Again." And this time he meant that the priest of each church was not like the priest of this church here.

"Osney, where I was a lad; the parson there. See him, a wild man, devout to hawk and hound, him. Great, tall, broad, lord of the manor, the roaringest man that ever backed horse or beat a sermon through the brake and slew it in a corner of the pulpit. Set to a hound he would any day but Sunday, set it to anything that moved, coney, hare, cat, rat, dog, child or bishop, come it wasn't Sunday. Sundays he allowed God was abroad ready to set archangels on him like hounds. Days of the week Parson Ramage hunted all and sundry; holy days he let loose a bagged sermon, cornered him up, killed him, and slung him a-horseback and travelled him out of church, dead, aye dead. Big, he was, and built like a tree, the bark against the bone. A red face he had, and a cheery one for company, freckled across the brow, shaved clean below, and dark hair lying forward, cut short with his own hand to stay it from his eyes when he was in the wind. 'Twas like being damned to go to church in those days, for he was a wicked man, Parson Ramage, just to see him walk you'd know he was evil and cared not a rap."

The pipe had gone out. The old man sucked at it for a time, then got slowly up and went into the house for another match. He came back and smoked, saying nothing and looking out over the sand and wild grass. Arthur looked at the same land, but saw something different in it; a tall stone church, clear against a sea, and by the church a tall man, red against grey stone.

"That should never be a parson," said the old man. "Perfect in wild-fowling, he was, and not just to shoot them neither but many a time to look at them, no more, so close he could take them by hand if he had a mind, out in the marshes there. There was marshes like it here one time, out the back there, that's why I come here, but they dried them all out, and dried out the birds too. But not so in Osney, one side and another of the sea wall. Many a time I went with him, call for me he would, stand at the parsonage door and give a great shout, right across the parish I'd hear it, and every bird and beast would nestle quiet for fear it was to be called next. So I'd go and carry a gun and a net and a great folded box, bigger than us both. It was our kennel, he said, and it strutted out when we came in the marsh and covered us so the birds never knew we was there."

Something about the way the old man held his pipe and moved it showed Arthur how big the box was, square each way so that two people could crouch in it, but not tall enough to sit up in.

"All day, like as not," said the old man. "And neither to eat nor drink or move, sinking in that marsh ground too, and those grounds full of the marsh-drench, the fever. Then we'd see enough by the time it was dark, and take our ways home to the parsonage with the box afore I could leave. We let the dogs from the church on the way; locked in they were when he wild-fowled that way, and the church the strongest place. They've eaten at the doors to this day, see any time. Then they'd run among the stones like spirits, and I never feared the hounds by day, nor for themselves by night, but low among the graves like that I was qualmish."

Arthur saw the night and the floating spectres between the

tombs, running off the frustrations of captivity, silent, bodiless. The picture was coldly stronger than the bright warm day while he saw it.

"He taught me to read," said the old man. "Not all would read then; and I might write too, he said, and sure enough I did, but he had no patience with folk, but I believe he would have taught a bird to read and write too if he found one apt at all. Every time I had a letter wrong he buzz me into a ditch so that I remembered. Q goes with U, I remember down by the end of a culvert where a lode went under the bank, this frog looking back at me and saying the letters, learned frog. Parson Ramage and many a frog, many a weedy water, many a bruise and ratching of a muscle, they teached me to read. Now all read, 'tis nothing to anyone, but then it was rare and no good thing."

"I read," said Arthur. "Write."

"Ah," said the old man. "Parson Ramage died on the sea wall, took at God's will without preparation, suddenly. He fired his last shot, and then no more. They took him away and buried him in his own churchyard. They say he runs with his hounds at dusk now, among the stones, but I never stood around to see. But I'm sure I heard him many a time after he died cursing and swearing in that church, as he used to, and seen him fly his hawks at little sparrows that was trapped inside. Just shadows, that's all. I was a lad then, like you, and I took colour from folk too much, like a damp cloth. I come out all streaked with the rest of the world, I fancy, when I thought they took colour from me. All the time I was a piebald fool."

He stopped talking for a time. Arthur looked at his watch and saw there was time yet to sit against the wall and perhaps take colour from that, as his grandfather might have done, colour and texture both alike.

"I thought I was a wildfowler, snaring the world," said the old man. "I thought it followed me. I laid hold of one of Parson Ramage's books and never parted with it, and I'll show you, boy, when it comes handy."

It was not going to come handy that day. After another long silence, in which Arthur saw again the landscape of the English shore and its tall churches and wild priest, it was plainly time to go home. Arthur got up and went, carrying with him all the way the weight of the wall he had leaned on; now it seemed to lean on him. Back at Aunt Deborah's house he went to the bedroom and pulled his shirt off. Mother came in then, to see what he was doing, and looked at his back with him. It was all indented with the impression of the weathered planks, knotted and grained and grooved.

"It will not harm you," said Mother.

"The world is shaping me," said Arthur.

A day or two later the old man brought out the book he had mentioned and showed him a passage, pressing the book on him with yellow hands. There was a long pencil mark under each line, where he was to read.

"Two fowls, called the knute and the dotterel, are delicious food, and said to be found nowhere else in England. The dotterel is remarkable for imitating all the actions of the fowler; for if he stretches out his arm, the bird will stretch out his wing, and if he stretches out his leg towards the bird, the bird stretches out one of his legs towards him; by this means the fowler approaches nearer and nearer to it, till he has an opportunity of throwing his net over it; and it is easily taken, especially by candlelight."

Arthur read it, and thought it must be true, since it was printed, and so long ago as well, because time was bound to make it true. He said so.

"No," said the old man. "It was not true then, for Parson Ramage tried it, by daylight, and twice by candlelight, till the wind took the candle, and the bird made a fool of him. But I was a bigger fool, for I thought it might be done, and I took it to be a rule of life, and that I was the fowler, and the world the dotterel, doing what I did back to me again. But at last I found it was not so; 'tis always the world that moves first, and 'twas I that imitated all its actions. And perhaps it was the same with Parson Ramage."

For the rest of the day the old man thought of the matter. Arthur thought of it, dozed, thought again, and went back to Aunt Deborah's wondering about Parson Ramage, now somehow part of him as well as part of his grandfather.

IV

THERE WAS a wooden box, with a door at one side, down by the marsh at the end of Aunt Deborah's yard. It was really the privy, or earth-closet, strong-smelling and dark, but it was the nearest thing Arthur knew to Parson Ramage's hiding place to watch birds from. He sat there for so long one morning, hoping that the strange bird, the dotterel, would stalk imitatively into view (and sit down, presumably, as Arthur was sitting, with hard-footed flies walking on his exposed flesh), that Aunt Deborah had to come down the yard and remind him that "other folk have insides that need attentions too, if you don't mind coming out of there." Arthur came out at once, and had to explain twice that he was not at all ill. But Aunt Deborah and Mother, getting together after they had had their turns down the yard, gave him a cup of bitter waters to drink, to cure any complaints he might have. His only complaint was not seeing a dotterel, or not knowing whether he had. Aunt Deborah said she hadn't seen any birds in a long time, with having lost her glasses.

One day they all paid an extraordinary visit to Arthur's grandfather. To make the visit possible they had first to provide the refreshment the old man would give them by making a vacuum flask of coffee. It was wrapped in a white cloth and put in a basket, together with four cups and four saucers, four spoons, and four lumps of sugar. Another white cloth was laid over the top. Then Aunt Deborah changed into a severely striped dress and black shoes with tall heels. Arthur did not see how she would be able to walk the sandy road between the houses without sinking into the sand, perhaps for ever.

The difficulty was solved in a way he had not foreseen. When they came out of the gate of the front garden into the road, instead of turning right and so on to the desert they turned left, and went into the town of Arnott's Bay. They crossed the line at the train stop, and then walked down the tarred road towards the main street. Arthur noticed that even on the hard road Aunt Deborah's heels left a print.

Once in the main street they went to the taxi office and hired a car to take them. A few minutes after leaving the house they were passing it again. The driver had grey hair cut close and the scalp below had blue veins below the brown skin.

The car smoked across the desert, and when it stopped the smoke fell down on it, being sand lifted by the wheels. At the church house the Preacher stood up, in his collar and shirt-sleeves, and looked to see who was calling. Aunt Deborah waited for the dust to settle and then got herself out. She gave Arthur the basket to hold, nodded to the Preacher, told the taxi-driver to wait, and led the way to the old man's house.

He took no more trouble with them all than he did with Arthur alone. The dog growled horribly, and even went so far as to stand up and advance on Mother, so that Arthur had to put himself between them.

"We come visiting, Pa," said Aunt Deborah, taking the basket from Arthur and setting it just inside the house door. She spoke loudly to him.

"I can hear you," said the old man. But he took no notice of the visit, leaning back and smoking in his chair.

"This here's Miriam," said Aunt Deborah, but he still sat and looked out over the sands.

"I think he won't hear or see," said Aunt Deborah. "Well, we can sit on the steps, I suppose." They sat on the edge of the stoop, because no offer was made of chairs. At the other house the taxi-driver and the Preacher were talking to each other, a rumble of sound with no words.

"Pa," said Aunt Deborah. No notice was taken. No one spoke for several minutes.

"I'm waiting for Clifford," said the old man. "Is he still on earth?"

"I should hope so," said Mother. "Why not?"

"There's none of his brethren," said the old man.

"He's at home, working," said Mother.

"I had three wives, one time and another," said the old man. "And naught left of any but for Clifford and his lad, and Deborah. She looks after me. Nancy," he added, as a correction to the name Deborah. He had done it before, but the other way round.

Arthur got up from his place at the edge of the stoop and sat where he usually did, close by the door to the house, leaning on the wall. Mother got up too, to come out of the sun. She touched the wrinkled wall with her fingers, and understood how Arthur had had his back marked.

Aunt Deborah spread out her hands, to mean that this visit was as hopeless as she thought it would be, but no worse. Then she got up from the stoop and went round the outside of the house.

"Preacher," said the old man, softly. He knew what was

going on but did not want to join in. Aunt Deborah had picked her way over the sand in her high heels and was talking to the priest. She came back quite soon and said they would have some coffee, and she would get it ready. Getting ready what was already prepared gave her an excuse to go into the house.

The old man did not like his coffee. He found it too hot from the cup and tipped it into the saucer. "English ways," said Aunt Deborah.

"Nasty fenny stuff," he said. "There's tea, or better, is more good to folk."

"I could never find the tea," said Aunt Deborah. "It's a fancy drink to me."

The old man's coffee was poured into the sand at the edge of the stoop. "She looks after me," said the old man, surrendering the cup and the full saucer. Aunt Deborah shook the saucer clear of coffee, meaning by the way she shook it that she looked after him if she could but some people you couldn't make any impression on.

"Nancy," he said. Then he repeated the name, and this time it was another correction, almost, because he meant someone else, not Aunt Deborah at all; someone much further away. "Nancy," he said.

So they left him, riding back in the taxi, not getting off at the house like sensible people but going right into the town and walking back from there. Arthur laughed to himself about it, and Mother too thought the thing so strange she dared not look at him in case she laughed to the world instead of privately.

"We might as well be seen," said Aunt Deborah. She knew what they felt. "Now they all know I do my duty by Pa, and if he says nothing all day worth hearing, then I still do my duty. I can see he can still manage out there alone; you can see that too, Miriam."

"Yes," said Mother. "But I wish Clifford could have come, Deborah."

Then they entered the house and separated into different parts of it.

Some other day Arthur went next to the old man. He was not sure of the order of things now. Sometimes, he thought, he and the old man were talking of more than one thing at once, or of things in a random order that sorted itself out for him later. Some of it sorted itself for him years later, but it all came to him in those few weeks on the Jersey shore, out of sight of the sea, on a creaking porch by a wafered wall.

"I was catching dotterel a long time," the old man said. "This antic and that coming on me; acting the my-lord-Ramage I was, inside me all the time; come-hithering the world; fooling myself it was being that simple bird by the candlelight of my own fancy. But I was just a boy, and you'll know you haven't had long enough to prove anything; it still might not be true at all, anything you see. Come a winter the trees are a shape you can't recall come summer; dying reeds on the marsh might never come again green and willing; some birds moult to the same plumes again, some to a different livery, and you can't know in the time you've had whether it will always be so. It was the same with me and the world: I thought full well that it answered to my dance through it. I was a fool. A fool in the long grass, when it was always summer, and a fool in the high snows, when it was always winter. I could forget the times between."

Arthur wondered where the time was now, for him; was it between, or was it one of the summers? Was this the moment that he was really being himself; was he himself more when he was walking across the sandy roads to this house? Was he himself most when he laid him down to sleep? Had he been most himself, most in his summer or winter coats, when he had been a small boy and the world smaller?

"The box was taken by the winds," said the old man. "Brasted out it was. I sat on the sea bank and watched the birds, being Parson Ramage to myself, and even then I knew it was not real; I was never him at all, watch how I might. I would be whole days, whole nights, out on the marsh, hoping to stride home and find I went to the church door and opened it on my greyhounds and let them bob and bow among the burials."

Arthur looked at his grandfather, and saw how the fancy went far beyond the possibilities. This small man, built light like Arthur himself, could never fill out the being of Parson Ramage, could never throw out a church curse, could never live for the wild chases, never hold the vitality of the tall, red-faced, godless priest. Some part of him he could be, because everyone can borrow necessary things. Arthur remembered borrowing an attitude from another boy at school. The attitude was to Miss Brenman, and it consisted of believing that she did not exist, like Santa Claus. Arthur spent several weeks in one term thinking she was not there, until it suddenly seemed to him that he wasn't there, that part of him was being swallowed up by the boy he had caught the attitude from. He gave it up at once, but he had already given part of himself away, and got in exchange this part that never, ever, quite thought Miss Brenman existed. But he had never got so far as thinking that he might turn into somebody else.

"How would you know?" he asked, when he had thought in silence for a long time. "Would you feel different?"

"I felt like him," said the old man. "Other folk would have had to tell me. Well, so they did, but 'twas another thing they told me. I was in the marshes one day, in among the great rushes, where the leeches lie, and you go in the sea after to get them off. I thought me alone, which it was best to be, and I swear the bird was a dotterel, though it comes more in the book than on the ground, and I swear I had it moving to my hand and arm, and foot and leg, coming together." The old man paused at this, and reflected, got up, lit his pipe, and sat down again. Arthur had him in mind, or himself in mind, standing in a watery place, with a bird attentive to him, watching with its sidelong eye, turning its head to read him closely, and approaching slowly, innocently, boy catching bird, bird catching boy.

"The bird flew," said the old man. "Every bird in the marsh flew. Every bird. And then it was full of devils, just my own mates of Osney and those I knew of Osney Cold Fen and maybe some from Battle too, followed me they had and watched and leapt out when I was most entranced with outdoing Parson Ramage, to be the best way of being him. So that was the instant I knew my dotterelcy was overed with, and I'd never be Parson Ramage, no church of dogs, no whip to smart the lasses that didn't drop a curtsey as I passed, or he passed. No, I was but Benjamin Thatcher, a lad from Osney, that had to work sooner or later, and would never be Parson Anyone, though I might have a greyhound if I wished, like many a lad. But I had been too proud to keep it anywhere but in the church. If you had wanted you might have known a poor fool that day, that sat weeping among the leeches, with his mind's sun clouded and his wits' snows melted, and his Parson Ramage storming off like he would storm off, smaller and blacker as he went, until, by night, there was naught of him left. There was no one to be."

"What did you do?" said Arthur, wanting to know the next thing because he could not bear to think of being in that marsh washed by those tears, with everything taken away from him.

"I went away," said the old man. "Not able to bear the shame in my own village. Those devils of boys that came on me, they knew what I had hoped, they knew what I wanted to be, and I could bear it before, not yet being, and I could well have borne to be him, but not to show myself being him no longer. I went away, north I went, to Boston, aye, Lincoln, full of parsons, a hill of them and the biggest church. And when I came back I had my mind full of my own things, my own goods, in my pocket my own money. So when I came I found my own father dying, with the marsh drench lying so putrid that year there was many carried their last time to church. I took that fever again myself then, and I remember what no man else remembers, when my father was laid down in his grave, that great voices came from the sky and carried him off. Those I remember, and the ground swinging, so steep it came as I went home that I took to hands and knees, and so they found me, on a level road, fast to a clod of earth for fear I should fall off the world and down through the clouds to the harder rocks below, and they sang as they flew home with me. That was the fever on me. And worse than that, which I can never tell, that came in that fever. The voices bearing off my father, and the world on its side, they were wonders, but the others were terrors, and no man should see those. But we had our cures, in the fen villages, which we could buy in Boston or Loddenham on a Saturday, and keep terrors off. By and by

I came well again, and took on that little land my father had from the lord of the manor, enough for us to fend with, after he took his heriot on my father's death. The best thing we had, the lord would take, at a death, and it was to redeem back and be paid for, in those days. Before I was well I was laid in the house many a day, idle, and then I busied myself to learn to write, and when I was mending I took a stick and wrote my letters along the shore, on sand, on mud, wherever it could be. I had my fancies then that God would write back to me on a cloud, but I dare not look there, in case I was found out again, as I was when I aimed for Parson Ramage."

"You couldn't be God," said Arthur, shocked that the thought could even be possible.

"God ain't no dotterel," said the old man, and he mused upon the thought. He lit his pipe. Arthur looked at his watch and had to go. "Be a bigger bird than that," said the old man. "More like a bittern. Them green legs."

V

THAT WAS how she had learned to write, Aunt Deborah said, when she saw Arthur the next day tracing his name with a splinter of fire-wood on the dirt of the yard. "Great A," she said. "The next one is B," but Arthur was not writing the alphabet. The alphabet is only an order of things without meaning, and the true explanations are found in its rearrangements and repetitions. He finished his own arrangement, then put the scratches back as they had been by smoothing the letters out with his foot.

"Writing is written for ever," said Aunt Deborah. "Don't forget that. Words are spoken for ever, and deeds are thought for ever. Nothing goes away, Arthur." Arthur saw it was true, because his name was still showing in the earth, in some different dryness of the morning's sea dew.

He went on down the yard, and to the privy at the end. There he watched the marsh, and was pleased to be watched back by an unknown water-bird. After a time he began to wonder whether this bird could be his dotterel, come to be taken. One marsh is like another unknown one, and one bird like another unknown one, and one wooden box like another unknown one, and one boy like another unknown boy. Which was which Arthur was not sure, and the water-bird was not sure either. Some time later, Aunt Deborah, growing impatient again, found him sitting in the privy waving his arms and legs gently at a duck. Arthur, seeing her shadow, merely thought it was Parson Ramage, until the fact that she was a known woman not like any unknown man brought him back to one local world.

"Are you taken with a fit?" she asked, with a sharpness he deserved, because this was the second time he had been in the way.

The duck paddled away round a corner of its green pool.

Arthur stopped being somebody being Parson Ramage. Aunt Deborah turned away and went back towards the house. Arthur followed as soon as he could.

"Now," said Mother, later, "that was thoughtless, Arthur." Arthur reflected that thoughtless is unthought, so it does not go on for ever. But it went on now for a little while, like a cure for dotterelcy. And just in case the scolding he was getting was not deserved, there was another dose of the bitter water to drink. That would quicken him, Mother said.

Some days they went shopping in Arnott's Bay. Once they went on a longer expedition to the end of the train's journey, one more stop, looking at the resort shops of the town front and eating fried chicken among the tourists, but not daring to go down to the beach, where every part looked private and regulated. Time came and went.

One day Arthur felt like more talk with his grandfather. He often thought Aunt Deborah would send down with him some useful thing for an old man living on his own, but she never did. He asked her about it once, and she said that he would not thank her for anything, or appreciate it; they had different tastes. He would remember how he had not been at all polite or thankful for the coffee. Arthur wondered why

Aunt Deborah could not have found the tea, in her one store cupboard. It seemed to him that she was being unkind, and he wondered if she was acting like a creep. The only remedy he could think of was for him to send postcards to Lorna Rackham and Maureen Taski, to fend creepiness off them.

That was for another day. For this one he went off into a sultry mist that had come from the sea, as it did one day in three. It was neither hot nor cold, quite, but damply tepid, unfresh, smelling a little like old newspapers from the floor of a cellar.

A figure began to take shape in the road ahead of him, as he went along, with mist moving between it and him. It was like a silhouette of a giant, walking hugely and alone. Then it was like a giant with his head floating above his body, detached but more or less in its right place. Arthur stopped and something thudded inside him, not only his heart but his soul.

The giant was suddenly close at hand, and had always been nearer than Arthur thought. It was the black priest from the church behind his grandfather's house, walking innocently and slowly along the same road towards Arthur, with his white clerical collar the same colour as the mist and separating shoulders from head. He smiled when he saw Arthur, raised a cheerful hand, said "You are a fine boy," and passed by. When he had gone Arthur felt that he had relied on the preacher to be there at the end of this familiar journey, not as a person but as part of the landscape. Perhaps his grandfather had relied on Parson Ramage in the same way, as part of the surroundings. Arthur went on, wondering whether to be a preacher or a bird or a parson, which is the same as preacher but full of differences.

The old man was in his kitchen, with the door open. Round

the house stood smoke from burning wood, because the stove was burning.

"That keep off the marsh-drench, the fever," said the old man, when he had looked firmly at Arthur and without saying or moving at all had indicated that he could come in. He went in to the hot, dry room, with its blue smoke from pipe and chimney. The dog, knowing him well now, stirred its tail and then seemed to expire with the effort.

"No marsh-drench on you?" said the old man. "Marsh-drench has been my life, for the most part. It bring riches, it brings sorrows, like the sea."

They both thought about the sea for some time. "A house like this," said the old man, and he let the remark rest.

"Such a day, just such," he said, and he went to the door and shut it. "But by and away colder. Before me, it was. We heard them the day before, but they might have been any place above or below. Maybe it was before the church at Osney Cold Fen, and some might say it was before Osney Cold Fen itself. But they was distinct from Osney tower, and clear from the wall by the sea, but the fret off the sea was like milk. Calling they were, calling all day, like a visitation, and folk calling back, and the parson, I know not what sort of man, called to them in tongues, being learned, and to God in church tongues, being learned in that too. We thought it might be birds, or lost angels, or holy children, calling all about us."

They sat in silence for a time, listening to the far-off voices of Osney calling in strange languages.

"If you were not there," said Arthur.

"I was a lad once," said the old man. "Aye, and 'twas before that again, and before my father's time that's dead. But I was there many a time. Knowing is being, and what I know I be. This was long before Parson Ramage. I was there as good as anyone. Now, hear the voices."

Arthur sat for a long time and heard only the bubble of the old man's pipe, the sigh of the slept dog. Then he sought his dotterelcy, the only way to join the old man's thoughts, by bringing the world to imitate his actions. His action was to be in that far-off place at that distant time, on that cold fog-bound day, and to hear the voices.

They were plaintive and despairing, and there was no way of telling where they came from. It was plain that help was wanted, even if the words were unhearable and unknowable. Some men had been on the church tower, but could not tell whether they were nearer the sounds or not. Others stood on the sea wall and listened from there, where the small waves crawled on the shingle and mud and lapped over the cries. Others coming from the marshes said the sounds were strange birds resting on some journey, whose gizzards, if they found them, they would split to discover strange roaches and seeds. But there were no strange birds to be taken that day.

At night it seemed there was a light far out to sea, and the bailiff of the estate came down to the village and said a fire was to be made on the sea wall. There was a difference of opinion about this, with men going from house to house and taking one side and another, and waking and crying from being frightened all day by voices, and hearing threats by night and quarrelling. But the bailiff was firm, and wood had to be brought and a fire laid on the parish wall. By the time it was done the light at sea had begun to fade and with it there faded the voices.

The villagers stood round their fire until the mist lightened without thinning, and they went home through a frosted stillness.

There were no more voices. By that night the mist lifted, that had hidden the distressed mortals or immortals, but there was nothing to be seen. There was only a flat sea, rising and falling in slow tides, and no wind anywhere. But there was a sunset lying inland, bright under the bare trees.

Arthur heard of these things, or perhaps experienced them. He was able to be there, on this warm day, and feel the cold touch at bare feet, the fire scald those same cold feet, the sea rise warmer than the air on them. He heard the voices come and go.

He heard the sea rising in the night, long before there was a wind, and men going out for a second time in the dark to watch the furious high tide. Before morning the gale came out of the east and brought the water high.

With the high water came burnt timbers of a yellow wood, not long in the sea, clinched with green nails, and one box holding other boxes, each one wet through and its contents of powder running into the next and staining the wood. The bailiff let the villagers have the wood for fires, but the box he kept, because it belonged to the king and then the lord of the manor. In it he found two gold coins, quite plainly heathen, and they were handed round for all to see, each no bigger than a man's thumbnail and hardly thicker.

I am not here, Arthur thought. But he let himself stay; and was it speech he heard from the old man, or was there some linking of real experiences? Whatever it was he could hardly bear the remoteness of the time when the coins were handed round, and was stretched almost beyond all possibility of reason by the feel of the coins themselves, and their burden of times and places still farther off, as if they came not from another place in the same planet, or even from another planet, but from some other sort of time, related only through the coins.

The bailiff took away box and money. The village took its driftwood and went back for another night.

In the middle of that night, in a close darkness, the man came from the sea. He walked in among the houses dragging a chain and calling out in his own words, that meant nothing to anyone there. He was naked, and his eyes glittered in the light that was brought towards him. He bowed himself down and the long chain rattled again. One end was at an ankle, another at a wrist, and from a middle link another length ran to a bolt that was driven into a wooden beam, but the beam had been burnt away, and that had been in the fire at sea.

He was locked into the church all night, under the tower, and in the morning came out trembling and jangling his chain, as naked as he went in, unashamed, strong, smiling and courteous. The priest came and tried a prayer on him in church Latin, but it was nothing to him. He had a different religion. When the sun came up over the sea wall he bowed himself to that and knelt, stretching out his arms, a shining dark man, expecting to be killed.

"With the sun rising over his backside," said the old man. "In the midst of the village."

Arthur was fully back in the kitchen of the Jersey shore now. The old man opened the door, and Arthur did not expect cold air to come in, and it did not; the mist rolling in brackish and wet.

"And never took marsh-drench either," said the old man. "Lived healthier than a native. He must ha' done, because at last he knew all our tongue and forgot his own. The chain the bailiff kept on him the best part of a year and then it was got off. I often saw it, when I was a lad, and never touched it but once." There was a long silence after that, while the old man looked back at some event, known only to him.

"Wed in the village, he was, and come a Christian like all the other folk."

"Parson Ramage," said Arthur, naming the only name he knew, and the least Christian, forgetting he might be making an unknown joke.

There had been no reply to it, so perhaps it had been a joke. Arthur went back then, into a thinning mist. He met the Preacher again as he returned, and they gravely bowed to each other in the mist, as if each had come from the sea during the night and there was no language both of them knew. There were no chains either.

"That boy," said Aunt Deborah, when the dinner time train had gone by invisible but heavy, "that boy don't smell fresh."

"No," said Mother. "It's the mist, do you think, Deborah?"

"No, I don't," said Aunt Deborah. "It's sitting cooped up with Pa, that's what it is, that old pipe and that old fire and that old dog, just like when I was young, and why I aimed to move when I could and why I did, in spite of everything."

"I understand, Deborah," said Mother. "But what shall we do about this boy?"

"Get a fire lit under the wash-boiler and get him boiled," said Aunt Deborah. Arthur was a little alarmed to hear that, because Aunt Deborah could not make jokes. She was not quite joking, though, only using words differently. She meant he had to have an extra bath, more than the one every Sunday or so, and that the extra would take place that afternoon. It was the first Arthur had had since coming here, and he was not sure how it would be. But it was simple. Water was put in the big sink in the wash-house, and he was told to get in.

Aunt Deborah came in with a pail of cold water. Mother was busy soaping him from the head down and made him stand up out of the warm water while she covered every inch, with Aunt Deborah standing by and watching, holding the cold water. Arthur was like the man from the sea, naked, unashamed, but not smiling because in fact he was ashamed of being washed publicly by Mother.

"There, rinse that off," she said, when she had completed each ankle. Arthur was about to sit down when Aunt Deborah, thinking she had been told to rinse him, stepped up on the bench beside the sink and tipped the pail of water over him.

"He's growing well," she said, looking at his shining clean form. "He'll be a man soon enough."

Arthur put a towel round him.

VI

ONE DAY it had rained, and the heaviness of the air lifted. Arthur thought he could see for miles, when he got up fresh that morning and went outside, but he could see no further than usual because of the way the house nestled down behind its railway bank with the pine woods not far beyond the marsh the other side. Everything he knew by now had come closer and sharper, so that further things ought to have been drawn into sight.

Aunt Deborah sang a little to herself as she got up. Mother and Arthur heard her the far side of the wall.

"First time she's done that since we came," said Mother. "I thought there was a canary in her somewhere; there used to be."

"She's getting used to us," said Arthur.

"She's lived alone too long," said Mother.

"But they wouldn't get on together," said Arthur. "Would they?"

"Who wouldn't?" said Mother.

"Her and her pa," said Arthur. "My grandfather."

"No," said Mother. "And, Arthur, you won't get along with anybody if you stop too long down the yard this morning."

"I'll remember," said Arthur.

There was a warm sun, now he was outside, a cool wind, and quick clouds bobbing across the sky. Now and then one would fly between him and the sun. He felt as if he could have run along in front of the advancing edge of cloud-shadow until the cloud gave up the chase.

In the morning he went out across the desert towards the old man's house. When first he looked towards the houses down in the middle of the abandoned beach they had been clear and close. But as he went over the sandy road they vanished and could not be seen, as if a tide had come over them. He had to stop and look again. They flickered for a moment into view, and then went under the tide.

He stopped, and puzzled. If there were no houses then there was no point in going on, and if the water had come over them he ought to tell somebody, but could not find any suitable words. As he stood and wondered he saw the explanation. A cloud-shadow had been moving across the houses and his eyes, used to the brightness of the sunlight, had not been able to pick the buildings out in the relative darkness. The shadow moved towards him on the south wind, and then swallowed him up in its turn, and flooded on behind him, swallowed Aunt Deborah's house and passed on again leaving it more or less where it had been before. He saw his own shirt being hung on the drying line, blue in sun, black in shadow.

There was no dog to greet him, or notice him. There was no chair on the stoop, and the kitchen door was shut. Arthur pushed it open and looked inside. The kitchen was empty. The other room had a bed in it, and a cabin trunk, and little else. There was no old man, no dog. Arthur came out again and walked round the little house.

"Bo-oy," said the soft great voice of the Preacher. "He has

53

gone," he said, "down . . to the . . beach. And there . . you will . . find . . him mending . . nets." His voice was full, his words were long and far apart, each one tailing off to a thread before the next started. All the tones of his sentence ran together into something like a tune.

"He isn't in the house," said Arthur, agreeing really that the Preacher must be right.

"On the beach," said the Preacher, flowing his arm out to match the flowing words, and extending his fingers so that in the minds of both of them they reached the water-side, somewhere.

"We will go down," said the Preacher. He went into the living quarters of his church and came out with his hat. He was already dressed in his tidy black suit and his white collar. "Now we are . . ready, bo-oy," he said. "Let us go . . . even . . unto . . . the Sea . . of . ." and there Arthur thought he had stopped, but the word 'of' extended itself for several yards of sand and then gave place to "Galil . . . ee."

"The Atlantic?" said Arthur.

"One deep . . calleth . . to another," said the Preacher. "It is . . the same . . . Lo-ord that . . made . . them . . . . all." And he ended on so low a note that it was almost beyond being a sound and was a distant vibration, like a train underfoot in the place where Arthur and Mother had had coffee on the way.

The Preacher smiled at Arthur with a smile that was beyond most other smiles, not an opening of the lips but a bursting open of the whole man, as if he lived only in his head. Arthur smiled back, but he knew it was moonlight to sunlight.

The Preacher led him down towards the railway bank, and then up the bank to the edge of the tracks, and then over them, to sight of the sea. Down there the water was blue, like the pictures of it. The sand was a grey yellow, but doing its best to be reflective and gay. On the sand there was a boat drawn up, tipped over to one side. Beside it the old man skeined and knotted at a net, with rising arm and bent head and blue smoke from tobacco.

"Thou . . Benjamin . . art not the . . least . . ." said the Preacher. Then he led the way down the bank and on to the sand.

This time Arthur leaned against a boat, in the shade, with the blue lapping planks making new marks in his shoulders. The Preacher put his hat in the bottom of the boat, ran his hand through the tangle of net the old man was tidying and mending, and sat against the stern. Soon he was making noises that were not words, long slow snores blending with the sea away down the beach.

"I had three wives, one time and another," said the old man, letting the net drop into his lap, because now he did only one thing at once. For a time, as a cloud-shadow went by on the railway above, he did nothing at all but look back in his thoughts.

"My dotterelcy was never done," he said. "Stalking the world won't work. It stalks back at you, and there's two sides," he demonstrated by lifting, "to a net, and both alike."

There was such a long rest now that Arthur was sure both men were asleep. But a puff of smoke, after he had abandoned hope of it, meant the old man was awake, or a very expert smoker.

"What happened to the gold coins?" Arthur asked.

"I've got past that," said the old man, after he had thought a while. "Terrible for questions, you are."

The Preacher woke up then. "Hey ho . . *Lord*," he said, and went to sleep again.

Arthur got up and went across the sand to the edge of the sea. Waves slid over each other towards him, different levels of water hissing on each other and on the sand. The sand ran about trying to dissolve. Arthur thought of walking in the water of the Preacher's Sea of Galilee, but this ocean with one restless fringe was not like the placid creeks of his own countryside, where there were fish you could get to either side of by wading or jumping. Here there was only one border, and that not very definite.

He came back up the sand, not disappointed with the sea, but not having been ready for it. He thought of being himself the man from the sea, washed up in chains from some flaming strange boat of Hungarians or Abyssinians or Tibetans, with a language all unknown. Being seen by Aunt Deborah was less than being the drowned stranger in a cold village among curious natives.

A cloud passed over the sea, like water on water, damping out an area of blue. Its edge brushed the edge of the land, a grey blanket lying over the lace edge of a sheet. Arthur walked on over the brown mattress of sand.

The old man was waiting. Dog and Preacher were asleep.

"I don't know," said the old man, "what came of the gold. My time was much later. That was just a tale, the man from the sea. But all the same, you don't know what he has to do with you."

"No," said Arthur. There was no possible way that some legendary man in another country and forgotten time could have anything to do with Arthur. There was only the story of him that Arthur could know, and the fact that he had thought about him and wondered what it was like to be him, not many moments before. Perhaps the old man had joined to his thoughts and borrowed them, in the way that Arthur himself seemed to slide into the old man's thoughts and memories or dreams.

"Folk came from Loddenham and farther, Ely they say, to see him," said the old man. "That's written, I've seen it. There was the miller at Osney Cold Fen took him in and showed him for money, until folk was satisfied he was no webfoot, and in every part a man and act like a man. Fishes grow different. He never took marsh-drench nor any fever, because 'twas mild here in compare with his own land. And that's how they come to be about in my day."

Arthur waited for an explanation of the last remark. The old man had jumped somehow, and it was difficult to know what he could mean.

"He wed this woman of Osney Cold Fen," he said, at last. "That's what it come of, and they've been there ever since, a family of them. They came up beautiful. Rare, they were, rarely handsome one and all. Not big breeders, and never many at once, one or two old ones and some younger ones, pretty people all. No, they didn't breed many, but what they bred they kept, for they never took the fever. When I was come back that time, and come to be the man of our house, I'd to cast round for to wed a wife. But of course I never looked far, because of Annie Lovink."

Just as some people say 'somethink' for 'something', so he said 'Lovink' for 'Loving', something that Arthur was not to understand for a dozen years, when he heard that kind of English accent again.

"They was all beautiful," the old man went on. "But Annie

Lovink was the one to by-beat them all. She was dark and lovely among all when I saw them together and just a lad myself. But when I come back she was dark and lovely on her own, and a growed girl, like old enough. It was the main thing I curs-ed me for in going away, when I come by Osney Cold Fen one time and saw what I'd missed seeing grow. Of course, Cold Fen lads never gave a thought, like lads never see what's next them until another fellow takes her. And besides, the custom was different. Well, I did love her so strongly, more than I can remember now, but I call to mind how I was dizzy with that love until only a few years since; and I came to be an old tree myself and shan't make no more new growth."

The Preacher woke, hot and glistening, and wiped his face with a handkerchief. "The Lo-ord makes his . . light . . to shi-ine . . upon . . you," he said. "Let us . . therefore . . be thank . . . ful." He got up and walked down to the water's edge, and could be heard making intonements beside the waves. The old man put on a pair of cracked spectacles and looked down the beach to him.

"I see him clear without these," he said. "Next thing directly he'll be down to the sun, all chained and mild, like him from the sea."

Arthur was about to ask a question then, because something important had come to mind, or was going to come to mind as soon as it had been made words. He hesitated, because he had already been told not to ask so many questions. This one never came.

"These belong to Deborah," said the old man, taking off the spectacles. "She'll have to get her eyes done again, they don't suit me no more."

"She'd like to borrow them to show me where you live,"

said Arthur. Then he thought they were both talking nonsense, because it was the old man's eyes, and Arthur knew where he lived. The Preacher went on talking to the waters.

"Take them on," said the old man, putting the spectacles on the sand.

Arthur put them in his shirt pocket, next to the watch. They were like an extra set of ribs next to an extra heart, ticking and sticking into him.

"If you go there," said the old man, "tell Clifford it's the custom to get a wife from away, and never mind being fussy. Then afterwards to take your choice, if need be. I had three choices, but never Annie Lovink, my Nancy. It was all set out with a woman from beyond Loddenham, that was to come one spring early, before the fevers began. But I wasn't one for bearing that, for I never saw her, and they wouldn't come down in the marshes and fens unless they couldn't prosper where they lived, so they weren't the best favoured of all. No, 'twas not my fancy; I wanted to court Annie, Nancy, but 'twas hard to go against custom, and my own mother, and an older sister, by a long way, that thought she might take a farmer from Loddenham way. So I determined to try, being in the middle of my dotterelcy, thinking it would go my way if I meant it to, and I waited my time, and had business in Cold Fen time after time, seeing her often but not speaking, so she knowed me and wouldn't take a fright. Then it was dusk one day, and I was coming back from the marsh ladened with my gun and a few birds and a hare. Then it was the right time. She was there by the house door, and none other in the street. Smart houses they were in Osney Cold Fen, not like Osney itself, which been there too long. So I put down my gun and the hare and all but a bird, and that I took up with me,

59

and she never stirred as I come; she might have been cold in her feathers like the bird in my hand. 'Annie,' I say, 'I loved you this many a long day,' and she said, 'Ben Thatcher, I see you look at me kindly many a time too. And I know you are bound to another.' And I was, too, by custom, if not by will, bound to Martha. I begun to explain, but she knew what I was to say.

" 'It can't be,' she said. 'We abide here, and folk bear with us, but we don't belong, and we look different, so dark we are, and we have to mind our ways, from when the first of us came like a captive,' and 'twas then she showed me the chain, hung on the wall, old and thinned at the link ends. When that breaked, she said, they might be free. I said I would break it, but I knew it was no use, that time wasn't come. So I touched her once, laying my hand against her face, and she near on kissed me, and I took away my dead fowls one and all and come away, for it was true, and neither of us could change it, not then. So there was naught to do but wait on time. Now tell the Preacher we can get up over the bank before the train comes, if he give up dotterelling the sea."

Arthur came to Aunt Deborah's house at the same time as the train. He gave her the spectacles and she put them on.

"Look at that," she said, turning about sharply, "Pa's gone and cracked the landscape with them. Well, who wants to see clearly? I say it's done too much these days, prying into everything. We'll see what we are meant to see, and that's enough."

VII

THE FRESH WEATHER continued. The next day the clouds were a little larger and did not move so fast, and they extinguished the sun more darkly. Aunt Deborah said it was coming in for rain before long.

"We can't have it fair all the time," said Mother. "Not by the ocean."

"You've been away long enough to think it's better where you came from," said Aunt Deborah.

"Rain's great," said Arthur. "If it's raining maybe I can sit and write those cards to Lorna and that creepy girl: I don't want her to get creepier." Then he realized that he had once almost thought Aunt Deborah was on the creepy side of existence and wanted to save her from it by being kind to Maureen Taski. But now, with being used to Aunt Deborah, and finding that she could sing in the mornings and not be fiercely tidy all the time, the problem was not so urgent. Perhaps everything would be all right for Maureen and Aunt Deborah.

"If you have the cards, do them right after breakfast," said Aunt Deborah. "It'll rain tomorrow, I think, so if we want to spend a dry day in the woods we should do it now, and if we want anything to eat then I need the table to work on, so you people clear out of the way."

People were glad to clear out of the way. Aunt Deborah

had a discussion with Mother about whether to walk to the woods not far off, or whether to hire the car again and go more elegantly several miles away. "That way," Aunt Deborah said, "other folks will hear of it and enjoy it too."

"The more the merrier," said Mother. "There might be some company for Arthur."

"They wouldn't come with us," said Aunt Deborah. "Oh no; they'd just hear about it and see us go and come, and talk. I think I'm talked about enough without being seen, so I might as well be seen, and you with me, better than anyone else, though I would like it well if Clifford could have come."

Mother thought this was an amusing point of view but not a very serious one. "We'll walk," she said. "All the way from here. And if we get tired of walking, we'll run. Now, Arthur, come and get those cards written."

But there were no cards; Arthur had not bought them yet. He did not want to write letters, so he wrote nothing today. "Tomorrow," he said. "That's when."

"Some lucky girls," said Mother. Arthur wondered what was lucky or not lucky in having cards from him. He also wondered what was lucky and not lucky in the way his grandfather had given up his Annie, or Nancy, and he wondered how that related to the way Aunt Deborah was called Nancy by him sometimes. She didn't like it, probably because it made her like a tombstone to have someone else's name engraved in her. He saw it as a picture, incised writing on a green stone: engraved on a tomb, entombed in a grave. He did not make it into words.

The way to the woods was through nameless orchards tamed into groves, then through a split rail fence and into the trees. Aunt Deborah said she knew some of the ways and went on and on confidently. But after some distance she stopped where the paths were no longer meeting or being, and said she remembered being lost for an afternoon once by herself when she was small and thinking she would die before bedtime whatever happened, to stop herself seeing the night.

"We can all shout together," said Mother. "But all we have to do is keep walking and we'll get somewhere. I was brought up in Kansas City, so I have an instinct for walking in straight lines; you can't do anything else there."

They were not lost, of course. They did not know where they were themselves, but they knew where the rest of the world was. Aunt Deborah was trying to become excited, that was all.

"There's another thing in these woods," she said, when they had found a place like any other place to set their picnic down. "Something I don't care ever to see. Maybe I won't tell you till we get back home, in case I spoil your visit here."

"There's nothing worse than Indians," said Arthur. "Like the ones behind those oak trees there. It's too late, they saw us," and he dropped himself carelessly dead over Aunt Deborah's neat cloth.

It was Mother, as well as Aunt Deborah, who was not amused. He was now streaked with butter, and the ants that had been in the butter, and had to be scraped with twigs and leaves.

"We'll leave you here," said Mother. "You always spoil an outing one way and another. The last time we went out I took all the time there was to make a nice out-door dinner and put it up in bags, when what does this boy do but come in helpfully and take out all the kitchen rubbish to the trash-can, so when we got there and opened up all we had was the kitchen rubbish and all the good food was rotting at home."

63

"You laughed," said Arthur. "I remember you laughed."

"No one would have laughed if I'd been there," said Aunt Deborah. "Disappointment isn't funny, and good food tainted isn't funny. That's two picnics you've harmed today, boy." Mother laughed then, and Aunt Deborah declared that it was getting disagreeable in these woods now, with one thing and another. They had to let her tell them without interruption about the monster of the place, the Jersey Devil, with its mysterious footprints and savage behaviour and fearsome aspect. But Aunt Deborah's account was dramatic and unreal; Arthur was not convinced by it and did not enter into the telling as he entered into the old man's accounts of matters less terrifying. It was not just that Aunt Deborah had not seen what she talked about, because the old man had not seen the man from the sea. Arthur had lifted more than the old man's words had told him, as the old man must have done when he heard of the visitor. Aunt Deborah did not believe in the Jersey Devil, so she did not see it with an inward eye.

When the meal and the story were over they rambled on through the woods until all three of them felt they had been far enough. Just as they thought that they heard the noise of monsters breathing. The noise turned out to be a few yards further on, and was the shutters being put up on a roadside stand selling ice-cream. Aunt Deborah knew where she was then, and bought ice-creams for all three. Ten minutes later a bus came along and took them to Arnott's Bay, about four miles. This was enough distance to make Mother sick, and they had to get off before town and wait for her to recover.

"It's when I get off trains," she said, "and on buses."

They walked home through the town. Aunt Deborah, it was not hard to tell, regretted not having the car. When they got home she muttered to herself, forgetting that they could hear: "I could have afforded it."

By morning it had begun to rain, gently. The ground did not get wet from it. By examining the yard carefully Arthur found that most of the raindrops did not reach the surface; they evaporated before getting there. Those that did land dried at once. Water fell in the marsh, however, putting rings of overlap in the pools, shaking the reeds and the leaves of other plants. The duck Arthur saw most days—if it was a duck and not a dotterel—was still there, unsinking, dry, as if the rain did not touch it either.

Mother had been thinking up a story about the Hooded Ogre of Kansas City, to match Aunt Deborah's Jersey Devil. She had told it at supper time; how it came up out of the city sewers and took people who were never seen or heard of again, including the Mayor and a visiting soprano come to sing an opera.

"No sewers here," said Aunt Deborah, treating the story seriously. "Nothing to come up out of. Though there was once a bat hung out there in the privy."

"Vampire, of course," said Mother. Aunt Deborah said she would make some coffee, and it was time Arthur went to bed, surely?

Mother came later. Arthur was still awake, with a thought ready for her, that it would be a softer bed in the mould of the forest floor. Mother agreed, but said they slept very well here, so there was nothing to complain about. "And," she said, "I think Aunt Deborah is getting more human."

"And more cross," said Arthur. "Sparking some."

"That's part of it," said Mother. "Being touchy is human, and I'm sure she's getting more like she used to be, or I wouldn't be bothering to tease her with Hooded Ogres of Kansas City."

There was nothing humanizing about the Hooded Ogre, in Arthur's opinion. The Ogre would eat people in the night, for sure, even if he didn't exist. But if stories about him had a humanizing effect, in the way that stories of wickedness in the Bible made you more good instead of more bad, then why not try them on other people.

"You know that old man," he said to Mother.

"What old man?" said Mother. "Where? Did the Ogre eat him?"

"My grandfather, of course," said Arthur, laughing to himself and at Mother for not knowing what he meant. He intended to tell her the thought he had almost had, but between laughing and listening to the new sound of rain gathering in the gutters and drainpipes, he fell asleep.

In the morning the rain had got itself closer together and was reaching the ground everywhere. In hard places it stood and sometimes ran a little way, but wherever it met the sand and gravels it went down into them at once. Arthur could hear it fall, and he could hear it being sucked away after it fell, a slight buzzing at foot-level. He went out in the morning with a black oilskin over him, head and all, tainting the rain with its folded smell and magnifying its noise with its firm panels of filled cloth. Drips from it tapped his ankles.

"Wet feet won't hurt him," said Mother. She and Arthur were going to the town with a shopping list. At the gate, however he turned the other way.

"I'll get the cards another time," he said. "I just want to go down and talk to him. He generally tells me things, but I want to tell him them for once."

"That's fair," said Mother. "He'd like a change, I expect."

The oilskin stood outside on the stoop, drooping in on itself a little but not falling down. Inside the kitchen there was a cheerful fire, and the old man was brewing tea. He offered Arthur some but he refused, because he had never tasted it, and considered it was a rather wicked foreign drink only suitable for well-grown people who would not come under its influence.

He began to tell the old man about the Hooded Ogre of Kansas City. He listened politely until Arthur had limped to the end of the tale. Then there was a silence.

"I ha'n't been further afield than Lincoln or Newmarket," said his audience at last, meaning probably that he had no idea what life was ordinarily like in Kansas City so that he could form little idea of what it was like with ogres. There did not seem to be a humanizing effect.

"Loddenham I went into mostly," he said, "and just the other side. She lived there, Martha, and we come to be wed at Easter the next year over. Not that I didn't go to Osney Cold Fen a time or two, but I never saw her, Annie, but far in the distance. So I come to be wed, and near enough got killed by it, for snowing it was, and a wind you could only close your eyes to, for I couldn't see into it, and cold like the back of winter. I come out of the church, with Martha by me, but we weren't familiar enough to hold hands, more like strangers we were. I come on the road past the church, and we had to be walking back to Loddenham, that was the way of it. She stepped back in, for to get a coat, being dressed to a spring wedding, and a wedding there was but no spring. That morning, she said, she thought it was apple blossom dropping past the window, but 'twas snows coming one after another.

67

Well, I stepped on the road, blinded like, when all at once something come slap into me and tips me over, then tramps on me four times or so, and then it lays on me, and face down I was, and this thing shrieking. They all come running from the church, and I sit up and see there was a young lady beside me in the road, and I thought, well, Martha, I thought, I misjudged you, you come out remarkable handsome once wedded. But it wasn't Martha, and I can't tell you who it was, for I never had the name, just the bruises. I'd been run down by four lady cyclists coming out on a holiday, and they never saw me, and I never saw them until they came into me. No harm done to them nor their machinery, but I got a broken arm, and I ain't made of pot, I don't break easy. Well there, I had to walk into Loddenham and doctor took me in and set the bone. That I never felt, along of what he give me to soothe me, something like the fever-cure, but a sight dreamier. So it all runs together, being wed to Martha and that springtime when the snow had gone and 'twas truly apple blossom coming by the windows. Those were days like none others, when all the sky belonged to me, and all the sea, and I had nothing against any man, and laid there watching it all, great and small alike, all equal; if it was a beetle, that was no less than a church-sized thing, and the young tadpoles dirtying the water was as wondrous as the sea monster; my own hand I might look upon all day, and what it was to me I would nearly know, and then the meaning would go; and 'twas a hundred miles down to where my feet stood, and there was new colours in the old grey blanket, and new words in the speaking of birds. I knew what they said then, but it never came into our language; that's too rough for their talk. Then it all went away, slowly, and the world was the same dry place it began as, and there was Martha that I'd wedded, and there was my arm with its bones wedded together too, and there I was, me, and nothing else with me, just me, to get on as I was able."

There was no more to come that morning. Arthur waited by the fire, and then went out to the clammy cold oilskin and settled it round him. He came back to the house and found Mother doing the cooking, and that they were alone for a while.

"Gone shopping, by herself," said Mother. "It's the first time she's trusted us with the house."

"What did she trust you to cook?" said Arthur.

"Something simple," said Mother. "Just for the first time: cold roast with a salad; I'm warming soup, that's all."

VIII

AUNT DEBORAH had bought guitar strings. She felt like it, all at once, she said. But that day she did not put them on, leaving them on the kitchen table and turning the waxy packets over now and then and sometimes holding them up to the light to look at the gut within the papery abdomen.

The next morning she was found in the kitchen, quite late in the morning, after the second train had passed, fitting the strings in their places.

"I forgot to call you, Miriam," she said. "Now, look at the time, and me not dressed." She was still in her dressing-gown, and her hair wrapped in a sort of nightcap, and her feet bare. The guitar, with the strings slack on it, made a mournful drubbing noise when she ran a thumb over it. "It takes for ever," she said, "and when it's done I don't know I can play it any more."

She was too shy to do any more than put the strings slackly where they belonged. One time when they were both out she would do some more at it, she said.

They gave her an opportunity that morning. It had stopped raining, and Mother thought she and Arthur should do some exploring on their own, and maybe get into town and buy those cards.

"It's a resolve," said Arthur. "Lorna Rackham won't know

me when I get back if I don't do something now. Do you suppose she has a romantic home life?"

"All girls do," said Aunt Deborah. "I used to have, I know."

"Not just thinking," said Arthur, "but really romantic like being from a strange family."

"I am from a strange family," said Aunt Deborah. "And so are you."

"Lorna Rackham isn't," said Mother. "Her father drives a truck and her mother buys groceries the same day I do, and if that isn't like my household I don't know what is."

"You're both very plain," said Arthur, meaning there was nothing strange and out-of-the-way about them.

"Homely is the word," said Aunt Deborah.

There was no shopping for cards that morning. Mother and Arthur found their way along the edge of the marsh and to a swiftly-flowing brook that came out of the woods and cut its way through the plashy mud and reedy tufts on its way to the sea. They could not follow it up through the marsh and into the woods, so they followed it down seawards. Its course lay a long way from the town, to the south beyond the houses where the old man and the Preacher lived, somewhere beyond the edge of the dry beachy bay. It poured along busily silent until it came to the railway bank, and there it went through a concrete tunnel like a drain, and was lost to them.

Arthur wanted to cross over and see it come out again and go to the sea, but Mother would not go near the tracks.

"You won't be sick, just seeing them," he said.

"If I don't see them I won't even be run down," she said. "And as for the brook and the sea, it's just water meets water and it's all the same a yard from shore."

"You are wholesome," he said.

71

"Homely," said Mother.

"Plain," said Arthur. "Or just scared. I think you must be a girl." But the girl would not come. Instead they both walked back across the sandy desert, leaving damp tracks because the top of the sand had dried and the lower layer was still dark with water.

"Do you talk with him a lot?" said Mother.

"He talks," said Arthur. "I told him about the Hooded Ogre, but he never went to Kansas City. He thought it was true. He doesn't like me to ask questions. Why can't we visit?"

"I don't think he wants to tell me anything," said Mother. "He never did want to. What does he tell you?"

"I don't know it all yet," said Arthur. They went past the houses and saw no one there. Even the dog was out of sight, and there was no smell of smoke. But as they went away there was a long quiet call of "Bo-oy," and a wave from the Preacher, when Arthur turned to look.

"They look in on each other every day," said Mother. "Your grandfather doesn't want anything else."

When they came near Aunt Deborah's house they stopped, not wanting to disturb what was going on. The guitar was in tune, and a thumb was being drawn across it to make different sounds come out, different chords and harmonies, coming and going without a particular pattern. Arthur thought it did not sound like very much, and why get strings if that was all that was to happen. Mother said that every musician had to practice, it doesn't just happen, and music is noise, so practising is practice noise.

First the chords were like somebody plodding over rough ground, knee deep in water, uneven and uncertain, marshy. Then there was easier going, and the walker could use either leg, left, right, left right, now and then, but the ground was still hard to cover. Then the road seemed clear, and all at once the music burst into a little trot of sound, swinging and swaying in separate notes, going and going. Then the walker sang a few notes above the running accompaniment, but tripped and fell and started again.

It was spoiled by the train, which came past and drowned the noise out. When the last coach had gone it had run the walker down; there was no more music of the guitar. Instead there was the tumbling of kitchen utensils and the raking of the kitchen stove, preparing dinner.

"We haven't heard a thing," said Mother. "She'll sing when she's good and ready. It's a long time since she did, and we'll have to wait for her."

They found her cross with herself for wasting time, though she did not say what she had wasted it on. Every now and then, through the delayed preparing of the meal, and through the meal, her left hand fingers stretched themselves over, seeking for the position of a chord, and Aunt Deborah listened inside her head to the sound as if she had just recovered from deafness.

The old man sat on the stoop again. That was better and more familiar, Arthur thought, than being beside a boat or even in the kitchen.

He sat down against the wall. It fitted him comfortably now, its knots and wrinkles were known to his back and shoulder.

"We're small things," said the old man. "There's no greatness to us, because there isn't anything but ourselves to see what we've done; there isn't a bigger animal, you might say, to tell us how good. At first I thought the world might care, out beyond Osney maybe, but when I went out beyond they didn't see me, one half the time. And in Osney we knowed each other, and my marvellous man, Parson Ramage, he was dead since I was a boy. God took him, in the midst of his wickedness, oh, the swearing man. God appeared to him, but he never appeared to me; you don't live to tell it. God's above me; he cares for a different set of things. When I was laid in bed with the broken arm it seemed that I nearly understood, time and again, and then it would be darkness or daylight or one thing and another, like Martha speaking with me. Well, it all went when I came out of that place and back to my fields again, working the same work that always was worked in them, and bearing the same sweat on my face. It never was any different there; only the lads and lasses had time to run about and play, and we had to bend and touch the earth to make it bring forth."

Arthur's back ached. It was not the wall he had behind him, but because in his mind he was bending over touching the ground in some mysterious way to make things grow, as Aunt Deborah touched the strings of the guitar to make them sound, one hand to hold the string in tune, the other to shake a note from it. It would be like that with the ground, holding it and plucking it, and up would come the soft sound of rows of sweet vegetables, the music of the fields.

"Good earth that is round Osney," said the old man. "But the land I had was too little, and we managed sparingly enough when 'twas Martha and me alone, and then when children are babes there's naught to find for them but an old wrap or two to warm them, and a babe will be swaddled in anything, it doesn't mind, and will lie and look at you. And Martha, she was a good girl, and kindly. But when the children had growed

74

up a bit, then were times we all went to bed pained with hunger, and nothing but dreams to live on. First along there was wildfowl to be got in the marshes, but the marshes were in Osney Fen Parish, and that parish took and drained them and put them in potatoes, lines and lines of them where I used to wander, and I could no more go there and bring home birds to eat, and the birds went away. Instead of the pleasures of wildfowling and drawing the hares to the gun, I toiled in those fields for new farmers that came to Osney Cold Fen. 'Tis no good, maybe, setting out to trap a dotterel with antics, but it might one day have worked. 'Tis nonsense to think of it with a potato; and potatoes was all we had where the wild birds were. If Parson Ramage hadn't been dead it would have killed him then to see the marsh dried out and ditched and drained. Then, one day I was in those fields thinking of other times, when farmer Marks, that made the land, came to me and said I'd done no work all day, because you see I was working for him, and that I had to go, and I was turned away without a penny more, and worse than that, there was no share of the little potatoes he didn't want to bag up and sell, because the time to gather them hadn't come, just early in October it was. 'I can get a better man than you, Thatcher,' he said. 'Don't come round here no more; I've done my best for you, but you won't work.' Of course, he was right, I hadn't done no work that day. But then he said I was idle, and that didn't suit me, for I'd spent the day thinking, and that's not idle, that's work, and there's thinking before understanding. So I up and aimed for him with a stick, coming in and taking our country like a thief and bringing abuse. 'Twas like the dotterel in the same place, with me raising a hand, and him raising a hand, and me advancing a leg, and him advancing a leg, match and match we were, and cracking our sticks together, and fist against fist, until it wasn't sure who was man who was bird, but at last one of his own 'taties took him by the leg and threw him down, and he laid there, and I reckoned he was dead, or if he wasn't that he'd have the law on me and thrown in the jail."

The old man stopped talking. Arthur felt himself being drawn into that long field with him, knowing what it was like among the potato stalks, seeing it as if he were there and as if he looked at it from the train. There was no escape from anything in the plains: he had seen that on the journey here. You could only go into the next field, where the potatoes are the same, one and another. But the old man was chuckling to himself.

"It would have been warmer in jail," he said, "if I'd thought." It was the only joke he made and the only time he laughed out loud. Most of his thoughts belonged to a more serious place, like the whole of the Bible, where they don't joke much.

"I went out of that field at once," he said. "I left him laid in a furrow, and if he was dead he could take root, and if he was asleep they could harvest him next month; I didn't care. I got up on the sea wall, and then down it the other side against the mudflats, and walked off. It came on me that I had to think, one way and another. So I walked all night, in the moon and the frost, and that was a change, with no Martha sweating in her fever beside me, for she'd took fever like they all did; and there was no children fretting and crying and clambering, and that walk was as good as sleep to me. Morning time come, and I was still between the bank and the sea, and the tide had been up and down. Next, as I came along, and it was all red was the morning light over the sea, I come on another land the far side, closer and closer it was, and I thought, there's Low Germany, and I'll be across and rest there. But by and by I could see I was walking by a river, not the sea, and the other side was England again. And by and by I came to a staithe, a landing place for boats, and there was a steamboat tied up. So I stepped on board and said I was a family man looking for work, and if the captain had no work for me would he take me on to any place where folk lived that might have work for me. He allowed I would have to work a passage, so then and there I ladened that boat full of market stuff there on the staithe. I was never big but I was strong, and spite of nothing to eat and nothing to sleep I did it, along with other lads to help. Then I got my dinner and a place in the boat and nothing to do but keep warm against the wall where the fires was. If you can remember being cold you can remember wanting to be warm, and wondering which was warm and which was sleep. That day or the next we come to a place and I got set off there. Bigger than Loddenham it was, but not so big as Lincoln, and it wasn't Low Germany by any manner of means. 'Twas Wisbech, I think. 'Twas far inland, wherever it was. Well, I bobbed about, like I had when I left home before, sixpence here and sixpence there, and lying where I could, until I got into some regular work, but no better than being at home with Martha, except it was quieter. 'Twas 'tatie picking in all weathers, and the rates for it no better there than at home. I got took by the month, paid at the end of it all, and I lived on raw potato out of the field and the dinner they gave us, and then I sent all the money to Martha in a letter, because I wasn't done with my thinking at that time and I wasn't ready to go back."

Arthur, by now, was ready to go back. His watch had ticked

round to the time of day when he ought to be leaving. At least, it had almost come to that time, and he felt he wanted to be home early for dinner that day so that he could come slowly up the road and hear the guitar being brought to life again. He stood up to go. The old man pulled at a chain in his pocket, in turn, and brought out a thick black watch and consulted it.

"I get myself lost," he said, "doing all these travels again. But they belong to you. Clifford never heard them, and Deborah, well, she got her house and if we get together 'tis like two beakers in a bag, we chip off each other's handles; 'twas always so."

IX

ARTHUR WENT HOME. The guitar was silent when he got there, but he thought it had been moved during the morning, and there was a sheet of music beside it, yellow at the edges. Aunt Deborah was humming a little piece of song to herself all through the rest of the day. Before he went to bed, and just to put off the moment of going for a little longer, because he liked so much sitting with his Mother and Aunt, he asked her to play and sing.

She said the instrument was not in tune, but she took it up and tuned it, matching string to string and straightening each in turn with the little peg at the end. Then she began to pick out an accompaniment. But when she came to the words the lilt faltered, she grew shy, and grinned too much to bring a word out. So, with the notes she had played Arthur had to be content and go to bed.

In the morning, before he and Mother got up, or were called, she clearly and definitely sang a song, though she had forgotten some of the words and had to slow down and sing 'La la la' instead.

"I can see how she'll be," said Mother, sitting up in bed and listening. "She'll be propped against the table like she was last night, and every time it comes to a difficult bit she'll duck her head up and down and shake it from side to side, and she'll move her whole arm to get her thumb to its right place again. Then she'll say 'Bless the thing,' and put it away."

They went on listening. "Well, be like that, then," said Aunt Deborah, giving the guitar a twang with her whole hand when it found one passage too much for it three times running. The guitar sung back all its threads of sound as it was put down on the table. Mother and Arthur laughed silently to themselves, because it was funny for Mother to be both right and wrong and Aunt Deborah to be so different and so exact. Aunt Deborah pumped water up and put water to heat for washing in.

Later on, the old man sat as still as ever. "I know where I got me to," he said. "That part I've told comes up like new to me, and the next part, I don't know what it is until I get to it and lift off the dust. I don't think over a thing just because it comes near me; no, there's times and places, and persons, and maybe here's all three. Well, the time come when I was bound to go back. First it was part feeling, stirring in me to be home again. Then I got signalled like. Now, all winter I worked on towards Newmarket, and sent money back when I could, and one day I was in Newmarket itself buying a Postal Order to send the money with, on account you can't send money in a letter, when who should I come on but farmer Marks.

" 'Oh,' I says, not thinking like, 'Mr Marks, Sir, you come from Osney and you'll be going back there,' because I fancied he might take the money with him, and save a few coppers.

" 'Oh, 'tis you, you villain,' he says, 'you that comes knocking down and murdering poor farmers in their own fields; I advise you to keep clear of me or I'll jail you, my lad.'

" 'Oh now, Mr Marks, Sir,' I says, 'I forgot about that little business, I got other things to think of, but don't jail me when summer is coming up.'

" 'Well, I won't do that,' he says.

" 'If you'd take word to Mrs Thatcher, Martha that is, not my mother, and this little money that I have,' I says, and I offer him those coins.

" 'Benj,' he says, putting the money away from him, 'I reckon you'd best come to Osney just as fast as you can, take my word for it.'

" ' 'Tis that, then,' I says, and he turns away. So I put the money in my pocket and set off back, walking straight out of town by Fordham and Ely and so to Wisbech and towards home."

There was one of the old man's long silences then. Arthur thought of him walking, in his memory, from town to town of England, some old England, on his way to Osney. There was nothing happening, in these long silences, that he could draw attention to; the journey would be like Arthur's over the changeless plain, made up of a dozen different things, perhaps, but repeated so often that they blended into one big sameness, where one part was very like another. Perhaps on the plain, and in England, the people were all the same and you went in and out of any house at any time and found everything the same. It would be very convenient.

"That wasn't the flood then," said the old man. "That come before or after. I was hedging it for the night, short of Osney I was, and the night too dark for travel afoot. But not too dark for the Fleetmen. Raiders, they are, coming from the other side of the sea, landing and fighting and making off with a village, all its goods and letting the folk lie as the axe took them. When I woke up they'd landed, and if I hadn't had a fever on, like we all sometimes had, I might have seen them sooner. Fleetmen they were, by the boats you can tell them, and these boats were run up on the mud the way they do. Big fellows with red hair, and axes, and they kill all and take all."

Arthur understood about this part of the story. What the old man had seen in his fever, or imagined, or had a vision of, Arthur could see with him. He was there himself, but not as a person with a body that got in the way of seeing or hearing.

The invader's ships were sharp menaces on the shore, their prows lifted, and the snakes' heads on them looking out over the whole landscape. The men from them had come quietly on to the land and spread out over it, knowing what sort of country this was because it was like theirs.

They found the village by smelling the smoke and the animals, and by hearing it wake. The man who had seen them when the first light came had come through the marsh paths ahead of the enemy and woken the villagers, house by house, with a word they understood. The men had come out and stood loosely round the houses, while the women and children brought out the animals and began to lead them away inland. Flight was the only defence, silent flight, and return when the Fleetmen had gone.

There was quiet when the women and children and animals had gone out of sight into the forest, to find their way over the marsh tracks to some place that would welcome them. The men waited by the houses, watching, listening, tending a small fire in which they charred and hardened long staves to make spears. Birds sang, and a peaceful day, with a wind gently from the north, began to appear in the world about them.

For a while there was nothing, nothing for Arthur at all. He was sitting against a wooden wall in New Jersey, not among the marsh village huts on their spit of gravel. Around him was the dry, empty sand, and the innocent forest was far beyond that, out of sight from here. The old man was silent again, pausing between visions. But he began again, whether in words or thoughts Arthur did not distinguish.

It was the same time, but a little later on. There had been one of those gaps where nothing happened, where there was nothing for the old man to draw attention to. The beginning of the next part was a distant shrieking shout, that began and did not come to its proper end but was cut off sharply, as if caught in a door. The men of Osney looked at one another without speaking, wondering. It might have been the cry of anything from the marshes, bird or beast, or the shout of woman or child. Or the trick of the Fleetmen.

Now the Fleetmen themselves were seen, picking their way through the sedgy places, following tracks that led them where animals could go but where men would drown. They came closer slowly, and then stopped, in sight but too far away to cause any harm.

After the one cry from far away there was no more of the unknown. There was a growing amount of the fearful, with the Fleetmen gathering all around in the marshes. The day went on, fair with a blue sky, a day that should have been ordinary and happy. It was peaceful with expectation of death. About the middle of it the men began to leave the houses, because if they did not they would be cut off from the forest and surrounded. Before they left they fired the houses and let them burn, and when the heat began to fail a little and it was certain nothing would be left, the men moved inland, to a mound with trees on, where there was a stockade already fashioned, not for fighting but for farming, from felled trees.

The fire at the houses dropped to ashes. The smoke lay over the marsh and over the sea, and its shadow on the land. The smoke grew less, and the daylight began to fade. The Fleetmen came up out of the marsh and began to kick at the edge of the burning houses. They were no nearer the men in the stockade yet. But in the dusk there would be a rush on to a known target; the Fleetmen had been able to watch all day and know how many they were fighting. The men in the stockade knew there were three ships but not how many men there were.

There was another cry now, from the woodland. A name was called, not this time the name of the coming enemy, but the name of one of the men waiting for that enemy. With the call came a small figure, running and stumbling over a field, running and stumbling and then falling and being still on the ground. One of the children, a boy, sent away that morning at dawn had come back at dusk and died a few yards away.

The men knew by it that the women had not travelled far before being caught. Without having to speak to one another they all left the mound where they were and went into the woods. The father of the dead boy picked him up as they passed, and that was the first blood they saw that day. They went into the darkening woods, and to a lighter place among the trees where there was a clearing and saw there what they knew they must see.

Arthur had come with increasing horror to this point. He did not want to see what came next, and he did not have to. There was an end to the pictures, to the sense of being there or of understanding the recollection or vision. There was his own self sitting against the domestic wall belonging to his grandfather. An ancestral home, he thought.

The old man was being silent now. Arthur was glad. He

wanted to wait, to recover, to arrange the new memories he had acquired, so that he could tell when they were to come and not have them flashing across his existence like the tail of a nightmare, remembered in the eyes and chest and hanging in the air after waking.

"Time was," said the old man, "lads and lasses would be going out on fine days in summer from work or school, to a field at Osney Battle, in the midst among the houses where there's a clearing. Then there was that game of the battle, that they'd always done, one day in Lent. There was one side of girls and babies, and the boys make two other sides, one side was the French, or Germans, or Scottish, depending, and the other side was the Osney men. The right way of playing was to get all the women killed off first, but that seemed silly sometimes, and proper other times, so we did it about and about, whatever suited. First off the men of Osney would be away at the feast, roasting a ox on a big fire, and sending the women away. Then these Frenchies would come and kill the women and come up and surround us Osney men, eating away at our ox. But before they could jump us out would come a boy they didn't kill, and creep across to tell us, and that was part of the game, one of the lasses would take the boy's part and run in or get by some way, and it turned out that the Frenchmen caught them all again one by one until there was none left they fancied, and they'd let them through. Then we'd all join up again and have the fight between the Osney men and these others, and rightly they should kill all the Osney men but three, and they'd to go and pierce the boats so the Frenchmen couldn't sail off. But in the game as often as not the Osney men would win without that, or all be killed. And if it was a wet day, perhaps it would never be played at all. That's Osney

Battle, and I've fought in it many a time with the lads, and I've seen it many a time as it was. I would often go there and see it again. Some folk have ghosts, but I have a battle. And not only that, I had many a place in those villages where things went on that I stopped to see and consider. Folk go to see where a king lived or a book was written, so they are haunted by those things even if they see naught. I was haunted by other things, and some I see, and some I didn't. And the more the marsh-drench was on me the easier 'twas to see."

"The Fleetmen," said Arthur, startled suddenly by the memory of them and their boats, coming out of the eastern dawn. His eye had caught some sharp prows rising above the railway bank—ships might be drawn up—but it was only the posts of the railway signalling system, and he had often seen them before. Now he was to be haunted by them, he thought, as if they were ships and he had been at the place where they landed, half a world away in space and time. The old man had understood what he meant by his words, "the Fleetmen."

"Nothing of it come here with me," he said. "Nothing more than I tell you. There ain't nothing to be seen out here in this sand. Ghosts don't travel like that. There's worse than ghosts in this country, so I hear. There's something in these very woods, maybe further south, but real enough by account. A real devil; they say there's wild country for a thousand miles or more, and then the sea again. And there's ogres in Trenton, a village a bit up country, biding in the gutters."

"Kansas City," said Arthur. "In the sewers."

"Ah," said the old man. "There's always things in water." He pulled out the black pocket watch and looked at it. "Now the train be due, and I'm stepping across to the Preacher for my dinner, and 'tis time you was off to Nancy's."

X

WHEN ARTHUR walked into Aunt Deborah's house there was a shriek, and somebody ran out of the kitchen into one of the other rooms. It must have been Aunt Deborah, he knew, because Mother was the person left in the kitchen. Yet the glimpse he had had of the vanishing person was not like her, and the shriek he had heard was not her sort of noise. She was too shy to sing and too steady to shriek. But she came back into the kitchen very soon and said they had forgotten about dinner so far, and Arthur would have to wait until something was done about it. Arthur waited.

"We're not hiding anything from you," said Mother, when she and Arthur were alone in the evening. "We were just remembering times long ago, before you were born."

"It's an old family custom," said Arthur.

The next day was Sunday. In the afternoon there was something very sober indeed. Aunt Deborah had been invited to call that afternoon with her guests on friends of hers.

"Quite wealthy people," she said. "Afternoon tea, no less; but I hope there's coffee instead." The idea of going on this visit made her solemn all morning. The guitar was in its case. There were days when such things did not appear, she said. Then she said she didn't want to go visiting these people. Not on a day like this.

"Nor do we," said Arthur, because he and Mother had discussed it and come to the conclusion that they would have to go.

"We all must go," said Aunt Deborah. "And we have to like it."

The friends lived the far side of Arnott's Bay. They walked there. Aunt Deborah was on high heels again, and it was easy to tell that she spent most of her time in bedroom slippers, now that she had got to know Arthur and Mother. She tottered as she went. Mother did not think high heels were suitable for long walks like this, right across town, but she walked firmly beside Aunt Deborah, only tottering slightly towards the end of the journey. Arthur just walked, in a suit and Sunday shoes. Every other boy he saw was racing about in a shirt and sneakers or even barefoot, sometimes on bicycles, always free.

The visit was all talk, coming quite often to saying "Isn't he like Clifford?" and taking Arthur's head and turning it one way and another. Arthur knew they were kindly thoughts, and that people who knew his father's life were part of the family history, just as much as his grandfather with his life story was. But nothing was said here, and all he learned was that he was like Clifford, and that everyone was interested to hear what he thought of his grandfather. All he could say was that he was very interesting, and no one wanted to know more. When they had finished with him, and when Aunt Deborah was out of the way, they kept referring to "Poor Joseph", and that meant nothing to him.

There was a small boy there. Arthur thought the small boy was lucky to be without attention, but the small boy wanted attention. He gained it by chewing quite a lot of cherries, something like fifteen, and swallowing the flesh but storing the stones in his mouth. Then, one by one, he spat them at Arthur, who was sitting opposite him. When he was sent from the room he would not go, and he had to be put out by the strong ladies of the house, spraying cherry stones as he went, and then spitting more at the outside of the window.

"Boys have such high spirits," said one lady, looking at Arthur to show she did not mean him.

"Girls are far less trouble," said another, looking at Aunt Deborah to show she did not mean her.

"Poor Joseph," said a third lady, who was very old and who kept taking a neighbour's cup instead of her own.

Aunt Deborah put her cup down and blew her nose. The other ladies looked at the one who had mentioned Joseph, because they knew it was wrong to bring the name out in front of Aunt Deborah, but they longed to have it out.

"We do sympathize, my dear," said one. "We always have."

"You must feel the loss most keenly," said another, "with your house full as it is now."

"Nothing, nothing, makes up the loss," said a third.

"But it's a very pleasant little house," said the old one.

"Nothing makes up the loss," said Aunt Deborah, and Arthur could not tell whether she was smothering laughter or holding back tears.

"Ah," said the ladies, and poured her more tea.

"I declare," she said, on the way home and safely out of earshot of anyone who could carry a tale back. "I declare I never drank so much tea in my life, and I detest tea. And they all detest tea, and here we sat drinking it. It makes me so dizzy; that and the high heels. And that little boy is called Nelson, and to think . . . well, to think . . ." but she did not say her thought.

Arthur was going to ask the meaning of the words about Joseph when Mother came to bed, but he fell asleep before she came, and in the morning he had forgotten the name and quite how he had fitted in.

Later in the morning he went out and down the road to the old man's house. The dog had been lying in one place for so long when he got there that the wind had heaped a small sand dune against its back. It had become so used to him now that it opened one eye to be sure it was no stranger and then closed it again. It was not a very seeing eye, because it was clouded like a pearl.

"I recall," said the old man, "that I near as anything never came to my children nor saw them again. For I was stopped in the street as I come, on a Sunday it was, early in the day, and the bell going for the church service like a tinker tapping a kettle, and Parson hurrying to the vestry.

" 'Benj,' he says, stopping of a sudden when he sees me, and any man could tell I hadn't come from home but from away. 'Benj, you'll come to my house a minute.'

" 'I won't, thank you, Parson,' I says, but he takes my arm and says the bell can ring on longer that morning. So we went to the house, where often I'd been with Parson Ramage and his rack of guns and the dogs like stone by the fire, and now 'twas all different for a different man, with books golden on the walls, and pictures of lands and never a stuffed bird to strut. This was a man that never heard of dotterels, a different one, this, with a carpet like blue snow and white-haired children tumbling like angels on the blue.

" 'Benj,' he said, 'we tried to find you up and down the country, before Christmas, but there was no sign of you, and you never sent word, and you ought to have done. My boy,' he says, and him not turned forty, 'you ought to have said where you was, for now I have something serious to tell you.'

" 'I come near the truth,' I says, 'as I came along, with meeting farmer Marks, that'll you'll know.' But I was racking with guilt, for money's not love, even if sometimes 'tis all a man can send. But on went Parson.

" 'Yes,' says he, 'a dissenter, a chapel man.'

" 'He said to come back,' I says, 'and then there was a dream I had in the night.'

" 'I can see that,' he says. 'There is fever in your eyes now, and fever means dreams.'

" 'She'll be beyond fevers,' I says.

" 'Yes,' he says. 'It beats all, Benj, it beats all. Ever since I came here I've buried one or two new-come wives each winter, and before I knew it the same men come round with new wives, easy come and easy go,' but of course he said it more like a parson.

" 'You should know a custom when you see it,' I tell him; for I wasn't alone in not taking the wife of my first choice. No, see, the custom is to take a wife from the hills, if she brought in some property with her, and even if not, like Martha, 'twas the same, they die of the fever in a very few years, not lasting them out more than four or five at the most. Then we get another, and so it goes, and maybe at the last, for the third time, we take from nearby the one we fancy, and she won't die of a fever, though she may languish a bit, times.

" 'Well, my boy,' says this young Parson again, 'I see you know all there is to know, and I have saved you nothing; and now I must go to service or the clapper will come off the bell and we shall be drowned.' And off he went, being quite right

91

about the clapper of the bell; when that comes off we're to drown. But that's another time."

Arthur began to feel how today's wind had carved the wood of the house into such shapes. It was bringing sand from the dry beach and trying to carve him in the same way. When the old man began one of his silences Arthur moved from his usual place and sat just inside the kitchen door.

"We've weathered to that," said the old man, sitting where he always sat. Arthur could not tell how he had weathered at all, being covered from neck to wrist and ankle, no knees showing, no arms bare. The rest of his skin was perhaps like his face, the colour of wood.

"I nearly turned about then," said the old man, "and walked off to Liverpool and landed here years earlier, and how that might have been I don't know. But when I had followed Parson out of the house and seen him off to church I could not tell what to do. One of the things I thought was whether the time had come to see about Annie Lovink and whether her chain had worn through and she be mine, if she still stood free. But it wouldn't be any good telling an up-country Parson about that, because it stood to reason he wouldn't be long here himself; the first touches of fever and he would be off to a healthier place. Parson Ramage used to say that if he took a fever he would be off to a better hunting-ground. He said, they call them livings where they put Parsons, so he ought to stay alive. But God is not mocked, and took him for other reasons and by other means than fever, and spared some poor parish his wild ways; aye, and spared Parson Ramage from some of them too. Me, standing there that day, I was a long way from being the shadow of Parson Ramage, and there was no dotterelcy left in me, no none at all.

"I went home, and my own children cried at me, not knowing who I was, Thomas, John, and Jane, and my own mother soft with fever, though not to die, being a Osney girl; and never a way to manage. So I sat in the doorway and wept with them, for there was naught I could do, and no present or fairing had I for them, but round money, and they knew nothing of money, so small they were. And besides, the fever took me again, that had risen in me when I came to the marshes again. So I saw terrors in the fever, and cried out so that they took my money and sent to Loddenham for the cure that comforts and gives sweet dreams to man and babe alike, and so we were quiet for a time.

"But there was worse to come, when I had wakened and the fever left me a little, except that my bones would ache and be like lead against my sleeves. This worst was, that I had missed the Michaelmas rent, last September, and meant to pay it in October, but went off wandering before then, thinking I had killed farmer Marks and could never come back. So, the fact of the matter was, I had lost the house. And I had lost my lands too, for when I was come into them after my father had them I had no money to pay the fines to the lord of the manor, and Martha had paid them, and so the land was in her name. But one way and another it was only part paid, and now it had all gone back to the lord of the manor, and I had neither house nor land, nor work, and three children to bring up alone. So I laid there, too heavy to walk, and the day drawing nigh when I was to quit the house for the hedges. And if I saw Martha she had nothing to bring me, for she was a fancy of the mind, who had been dead since a week after Christmas. And the apple blossom fell all spring past the window, like snow at Epiphany."

He stopped speaking. Arthur looked down and saw the sand hurrying across the stoop, eating at the wood but burying it at the same time, just as snow at Epiphany had buried Martha.

It came to him clearly that Martha had been one of his grandmothers. The time of her burial had not been in his lifetime, but if Martha had lived she could have been sitting here now; yet they were telling tales about her as if she had never been real to anyone living, like a king or queen of ancient times. Martha was dead, but she had lived, and the old man a few feet from Arthur, his grandfather, was his link with her.

"I'll go now," he said. He wanted to be alone with his thoughts about Martha. The babies, Thomas and John and Jane, were his uncles and aunts, just as Aunt Deborah was an aunt. They were aunts and uncles too young to understand money. He tried to belong to them as they belonged to him, but it was difficult to be there, and the idea of them all went away as a gust of wind licked the backs of his knees with sharp fast sand and hastened him on the way home.

In the afternoon he and Mother went shopping while Aunt Deborah finished her washing of clothes. They were drying quickly out in the yard, but coming in gritty. She said she had to put up with that some days in the year. It was fog, or grit, or railway smoke.

They meant to buy cards for Lorna Rackham and Maureen Taski, but when they were coming towards the shop, on the way home, they saw one of yesterday's ladies leading yesterday's little boy into it.

"We won't," said Mother. "Your girl-friends will have to wait another day. They've probably forgotten you already."

"I hope so," said Arthur. "I sincerely hope so," but he did not care at all.

The little boy came out of the shop alone, with his cheeks bulging.

"Look out, Mother," said Arthur, because red cherry stones would mark her coat. But the little boy had no cherry stones today; he had a mouth full of air, and was having a joke. It was not a very funny joke, whoever played it. Mother did not laugh. The little boy dredged up a small amount of wet spit and spat that at Arthur from much too far away. Arthur raised his hand, and the little boy fled into the shop.

"They're so sweet at that age," said Mother. "If they belong to someone else. If other people's children were brought up right they'd be perfect; it's one's own that are hopeless. You spat tomato soup at me once. You did it deliberately."

"I remember," said Arthur. "It was before I knew about money, a long time ago."

XI

ARTHUR WAS standing beside the railway track at the station the next morning, on his way to the town to buy the cards he wanted to send. He had forgotten the reason for sending one to Maureen Taski but had remembered his promise to send Lorna's. About them both he had a feeling that he knew was nonsense; that if he did not send them cards now, at once, then they might be put out of their houses, as if the cards were a sort of rent. He was working on the nonsense when a hand came on his shoulder, gentle and large, and a deep voice said, in a questioning way: "Bo-oy?"

It was the Preacher, walking about as Arthur had been. The hand stayed on Arthur's shoulder and they began walking together. "We must . . praise . . the Lo-ord . . . for . . this . . . bea-utifu-ul weather . ." said the Preacher, showing with his other hand the blue sky, and stroking with its palm the small wind coming along the coast. "Do yo-ou . . . Praise the Lo-ord, bo-oy?"

"Sundays, if we get to church, I do," said Arthur. It was not what he wanted to say. He wanted to tell the Preacher, clamped to his shoulder now, that he had been walking towards the town, not away from it as they were now. But he thought it might be difficult to mention it, and in any case it was the sort of thing that would amuse Mother, to hear how he had stood still for a moment and in that moment had been turned round by the hand of the Preacher, like the hand of God.

"The church . .," said the Preacher, "is . . ri-ight the-ere . ." and he pointed ahead, beyond Aunt Deborah's house and across the sand. "Sunday, or Monday, or Tuesday or any . . day, they a-all . . belong to . . the Lo-ord."

"Mother isn't sure about all that," said Arthur.

"Never you mi-ind," said the Preacher, and his hand seemed to grow larger on Arthur's shoulder. "Never you mi-ind, bo-oy; the Lo-ord is sure, and . ." and he dropped his voice to a rumbling shadow of a whisper, "the same . . . Lo-ord is . . merciful."

"I'll tell her," said Arthur. Then they were by the gate of the house. Arthur paused himself without stopping, and the Preacher understood that he was going in at the gate and released him. Arthur stopped walking then. The Preacher stopped as well and turned round.

"I was going . . into town when I saw you . . coming . . back," he said, "so I turned and came . . back . . with yo-ou. The Lo-ord be . . with yo-ou."

"And with thy spirit," said Arthur, knowing the words from somewhere. They were the right ones. The Preacher smiled at him, rumbled in his throat and chest, which was the voice of the smile, and walked off towards the station again, the way Arthur had been going.

Arthur was about to go into the house again when he heard Aunt Deborah, inside it, saying that there was no one in but themselves, Miriam, and keep an eye open for the Preacher, we don't want him hearing us, and the guitar began to twang. Arthur knew it would stop if he went in, so he stayed outside.

It was obvious that the world was against going into Arnott's Bay that morning. Instead he walked out across the sand towards his grandfather's house.

Out in the waterless places, where the sand was softest and the slopes of it slid underfoot, he came on the grave. It had been there a long time, as if a dog had gone to sleep and dreamed itself to a skeleton, lying there peacefully, half covered with the warm sandy quilt. Its old teeth were locked in a smile that showed it would not bite; its paws were curled under the longer bones of its legs; its back was bowed reposefully. It was not dead in any alarming way, but resting, waiting to get up at a call and go off on some new hunt or walk in the next existence it would have.

Arthur bent and touched a white clean bone. His hand was heavier than the touch of sand and wind had been, and the bone he touched, on the fallen shoulder, made it fall even more, with a hollow rattle. He thought then that he had spoilt the dog, perhaps for ever, and tried to set the bone back where it belonged, dribbling sand in behind it to make it stand as it should. Then, when he had done that, he smoothed new dry sand over all and walked round the grave and went on. He forgot his straight line and went in the general direction of the houses until he stood among them and knew which was which.

The old man was sitting watching the sand. His dog lay just as the bones had lain, as if they had got up and come ahead and been clothed as people were clothed. Arthur put his hand down and touched this dog's shoulder, carefully. There was a mat of fur on this one, and under the fur a layer of hard fat and skin, and no bone with white edges. The dog took no notice of him. There was no more bite in him than there had been in the skeleton.

"What's he called?" said Arthur.

"Master," said the old man. "Your grandmother named the first dog I had, and I called them all the same since, Master."

"Not Martha, that was too long ago," said Arthur.

"Florence," said the old man. "When I came to New Jersey. That was a time ago, and there's been three or four Masters by my side. Come they die I bury them out in the sand yonder."

"I found one," said Arthur, knowing at once that he had.

"I've done that too," said the old man. "Time changes them. Time changes many things, but it changes them so slowly that good things seem they will always be good, and bad things that they will always be bad. There was a bad time when I come back to Osney and Martha was dead without being grieved over when I could have grieved. When I came it was too late, and the new grass was showing on her earth. And that was all the earth I had that was aught to do with me, for we were put out of the house and we were shelterless. And there I was, just a young fellow, with no money nor much wits, and three children to grow. I went up to the manor house to beg for work, for there was only charity in the village, and charity is giving, not taking; you can't buy it or order it. She was high with me, was Miss Cartwright, that was lord of the manor then. She let me in, right enough, to the business room where I was to stand cap in hand, but the children had to stay out in the kitchens, where I put them cold as ice. Miss Cartwright didn't have any fancy for children, being just a single lady.

" 'Well, my man,' says she, 'what sort of a tale have you to tell? I'm bound to say there isn't much I can do for you, because you brought it upon yourself.'

" 'I'm no idler, Miss,' I says, 'I went away, but I worked when I was away and I sent money back.'

" 'That wasn't plenty,' she says. 'You owed me money, and you owed me work, for you're my tenant. You still owe me money, Thatcher, and 'tis writ in this book. And this is not the first time you've wandered off unaccountably; you did it once before,' and so she did go on, until at last she gave me half a crown, and sent me out again.'

"Half a crown," said Arthur, picturing a sort of hat.

"Money," said the old man. "Just the one coin. But they say charity begins at home, and I had no home. So I left the coin where she set it, on the table, and came out and went back to my sister's house and told her of it. So she got straight up and went to her ladyship and took the half crown from her and brought it back with the children too, that had been warming in the kitchen at the manor house, along with Miss Cartwright's housekeeper to carry one of them. Edith was her name, and she'd taken the children in by the fire and tended them and plied them with food, and that was like love for them, which they never had from my sister and not from me that was shiftless and could never provide. So I took the money and gave part to my sister and kept part, and with that part I would walk to Loddenham when my bones grew heavy and buy the Indian flowers out of the apothecary's shop, and so give me peace that summer. It seemed to me I ought not to love what I could never care for, so I went out and lived by the edge of the marsh, and was good for nothing, coming in the day to the manor house to beg for food for the children, and that good Edith keeping somewhat aside each day. Then I would go into Osney Cold Fen and perhaps see Annie Lovink, and she had no man just as I had no woman, and the chain that came off the man from the sea still hung up entire on the house wall. Once I looked full at her in the road, but she turned away. Maybe if I had taken one more step she might have looked towards me again, but I turned away too, seeing that I was no sort of a man any woman would take. Lying out there in the marsh I would dream of hope, and when I was dreaming 'twas all well and bright, and when I woke 'twas the grey summer of the coast and I would shake like a fever. One day, in these shakes I came up to the manor house, and Edith took me into the kitchen, against the fire, like I was a babe myself, while she wrapped a paper of broken meats to take to the little ones. Miss Cartwright came in the kitchen then, and she was high with both of us.

" 'What are you doing sitting by my fire?' she says, when by custom the kitchen isn't her fire.

" ''Tis the marsh-drench on him, Ma'am, that makes him tremble so,' says Edith.

" 'This isn't the poor house or the infirmary,' says my lady, and she come and pitch me out with her own hand, for she wasn't dainty at all. 'You've been taking Indian flowers,' she says, 'I can tell, and you was useless before and now you are worthless too, and if you don't mend I'll have you turned out of the parish and your children put in an orphanage and sent to Australia or Canada, and you'll never have the will to oppose me.' Then she stamps off to kill some other poor fellow, groom or cowman, or so. Edith comes out then and takes me up from the cobbles, and it came to me then that I wanted lifting, not dropping, and that Edith was a fine, loving woman, and I told her so. She didn't mind to hear."

The old man was silent for some time, waiting to see what he remembered next. "Which way to turn," he said. Arthur looked at the unmoving dog and reconstructed in his mind the bones that must lie within it. All he could see of the skeleton was the black margin of some upper teeth and the yellow smoothed edges that the grains of time had worn away.

"We might have got wed," said the old man. "But if we had Miss Cartwright would have sent Edith away, we knew that. And all the house she had was up at the manor, and I wasn't allowed in. Then I found work here and there and gave part to Edith and part to my sister, and none to me for Indian flowers, unless the marsh-drench was too much for me. Then there came a day when Edith wasn't out by the stableyard gate just at the time we fixed, and she never came, and I don't know what I felt, for if she had given me up then I knew that nothing had changed in me, I still had the same head and arms and legs and very near the same thoughts, so all was near the same; and if she was never to come again then I was free. But if she came now before I went, then I would not have changed either. So it seemed to me that the world changed on its own, and I stayed the same, and perhaps that was the end of my dotterelcy. But she came, at last, and still I knew not what to think, glad or sorry, for her father that lived in Cold Fen had died and she had come into a house and land, and at the very least wanted a man to work it at once in this haymaking season and fruit close by, and nothing of a husband needed for her, just a man for the land. Well, 'twas all, the crown of our needs, house and home, and meat and drink, and all to walk into. So I walked over there that evening about eight by Osney clock and came into that warm house where he was laying, her father, and looked out the work to be done, the hay sweet in the fields, and the cow full of milk, and eggs in the yard, and I managed full ten times as well as I ever did in my life. One thing, though; the house standing opposite Annie Lovink's, and that was the only disturb in the whole matter. And of course, I hadn't time to think, first away, with the work to be done. And then Edith and I came to be married. No church ever was at Osney Cold Fen, just a chapel, and no parson with pretty ways and cold heart, such as we had then at Osney that never let me do what Parson Ramage did for his dogs, sleep in the church with my shelterless children.

"'We'll have to wed,' says Edith, 'for as it is I can't sleep at my own house any night of the week with you in it, Benj, and I could when my father lived in it, and even more I should when 'tis my own.' So we come to it, and then we brought the children, and 'twas for me like being a boy again, among my own, and no cares but the one, that Annie Lovink I still hanker for, across the road, and see her many a time, and that chain. If that chain broke I don't know what I might do, but it never did. And there I was happy twice and many more times, a proper market-going farmer. Miss Cartwright, like her sort, was still high with us, and she couldn't mean any good wishes to me that took Edith away. But if she had left me my house I would have left her her Edith, I reckon. She spited herself, when it come to it."

XII

ARTHUR CAME back to Aunt Deborah's house hoping to burst in on a full session of guitar music. But no sounds of plucked strings came forward to meet him along the sandy road. The house was still. Arthur stood and listened to the quietness, sheltered from the wind under the railway bank. He tried to persuade sound to come across the air to him, but there was no sound to come. He left the listening behind him and went indoors.

"Well, that's enough of that," said Aunt Deborah, leaping up from the kitchen chair she was sitting on. The chair scraped across the floor the other way, because she had got up so suddenly. The chair stopped moving, but its noise of wood on wood went on. The continuation of noise was Aunt Deborah blowing her nose. When she sniffed Arthur knew it was no longer the chair. He felt that some story-telling had been going on here while he had been hearing other stories further down the road.

"It was a long time ago," said Mother. For a moment Arthur did not know what she could mean, because she had not been there when his grandfather had been telling him that life-story. That had been a long time ago. But Mother meant Aunt Deborah, and a different long time, and a different ago.

"Some things you take with you," said Aunt Deborah, dabbing with a kitchen cloth at the corner of an eye where a tear was still living. "Some things you just don't get away from, Miriam. Joseph just never would approve of light music on a guitar, not on a guitar."

"But you are so good at it, Deborah," said Mother.

"Are you saying that if I am good at a sin, then I ought to go on doing that sin?" said Aunt Deborah.

"I might just say that," said Mother. "I might just say it isn't a sin to start with, so you can do what you like."

"It's just as if Joseph was listening and sending down messages to me," said Aunt Deborah. "When I get my fingers on the strings it's like plucking at his heart."

"It is your own heart," said Mother. "I say that we do what we want, and you don't know what you want. But I know what Arthur wants, and that's his dinner."

"We've been talking so," said Aunt Deborah to Arthur, "that we forgot your dinner."

"Joseph never could remember details like that," said Mother.

Aunt Deborah had taken up a knife by the sink, to do some cooking operation with. When Mother spoke she stabbed the knife down into the wooden draining board and let go of it. It vibrated on its own.

"I don't call that kindly," she said. "And it's no way true, Miriam; and I didn't ask you to come to be uncivil to the living and unkind to the dead." She left the sink, dried her hands on the cloth that had wiped away a tear, and walked towards the yard door.

"Now, you wait, Deborah," said Mother, getting up from her chair quickly, though not quite with Aunt Deborah's leap, and standing in front of the door until Aunt Deborah came to her, and then holding Aunt Deborah's arm. "That's no insult, Deborah. That's just to remind you that you do what you want to do, but sometimes you *think* what you want to do, and other times you just go straight on and do it, like we all do. You just know you have to give us dinner, so you go right ahead and do it, and you wouldn't dream of asking for Joseph's permission, for any of those things, because you know he hasn't anything to say about them. You aren't living your life for him, Deborah, not most of the time, you know you aren't. All that's a long time gone, and there's plenty to do since then. You need to be free, and get your spectacles mended and look out more clearly on the world."

"I'm sure I don't know a word you mean," said Aunt Deborah, pulling Mother's hand away and edging her way to the door. "But I declare you upset me, Miriam, and I'm going down the yard, because I have my bowel complaint coming on again." She went out of the yard door and closed it after her.

"You're not always just like my mother," said Arthur, when he had considered the unusual behaviour of both of them.

"No," said Mother. "Just then I was your Aunt Deborah's sister-in-law. That's what I came to be. Now I'll have to be cook, and get on with the dinner." She pulled the vibrating knife out of the wood by the sink, and cut cold meat with it.

They were eating it when Aunt Deborah came in. She said nothing, and sat at the table and ate her dinner. "Are you all right?" said Arthur politely, after a while.

"It was a false alarm," said Aunt Deborah. "My insides aren't so capricious as they used to be and I was wasting my time down there, so I came back. I was just sulking, and the flies were monstrous." She was cheerful again, it seemed. "It's going to tea with those folks of his," she said. "That sets me back a bit. They always make me feel guilty at having this house and all I live on, but they don't need it, no not at all." While she washed the dishes she sang snatches of song, quietly.

After that Mother wondered whether Arthur could find something else to do for the rest of the afternoon. She had meant to go out for a walk with him, but she thought she should stay and talk to Aunt Deborah. Arthur wanted to go for the walk and hear about Joseph and who he was, and why Aunt Deborah wasn't perfectly happy with a house and a guitar and nothing to worry about.

Perhaps though, he thought, people have to worry all their lives, not just at the age Arthur was himself. His only worry at the moment was the one about the postcards, and it had to remain a worry, because now he was outside the house and had no money in his pocket. Instead of going towards the town and possibly being turned round by the Preacher, he went towards the three houses put in the sands.

This morning he had walked in a straight line and failed to keep an eye on the buildings; they had moved about, either in his mind or really, and he could not tell which was which. This afternoon he set out towards them, following the road, and keeping just one of them firmly in sight, so that he was bound to know where it went as he journeyed.

Once more he failed to keep the right one identified. He found he was muddled when one house went behind another, and he could not tell which had come out which side. He was walking backwards and forwards in the road, until he tripped over a tussock of grass and went flat on his back. When he got up the houses had danced away.

"Dotterelcy," he said to the sand and the sky. "Dotterelcy," and he jumped about in the road, waving arms and legs, until he was sure nothing was obeying or disobeying him. None of the objects he could see took any notice at all, and that was normal.

The old man was gently asleep. The dog lifted its head and looked at him, at Arthur, at its own hind foot, and went to sleep itself. Arthur stayed on the soft sand outside the stoop for a while, then went for another walk round the houses. There was no one here but his grandfather. The Preacher was absent.

The old man had woken when he got back. The only difference was that his eyes were open, not shut. Otherwise he had not moved.

"Settled," he said, when Arthur had come up and sat against the worn wall. "You come visiting this summer, and I shan't see you no more after you leave, so you might hear all. I minded to tell you of the marsh by Osney Cold Fen. Part was taken up in potato fields, but part was just as it began, not a potato near it, over beyond the sea wall. There I went as a lad, there I went with Parson Ramage, and there I might go as a farmer with my own gun to bring back game for my own children and Edith and those two of our own we had, and maybe something for her across the road. She'd a little one of her own then, the same as they did, the Lovinks, they just come by a girl like themselves each time, no trouble about husbands or getting wed. Well now, 'twasn't my get, that babe, but it growed alongside mine. Now there were days when it might be a holiday and a fine day too, out of the shooting season, when I would be on that marsh. There's Thomas, he's a grand sprightly lad being then about twelve years old, and his full brother John, the year less in age, and not so steady perhaps, ready to quarrel and follow any dazzler, like his Dad had been, and then his full sister Jane, which had a round face and long yellow hair and being about ten years old at the same time, and still one for questions, why and why and when, and then a half sister, Sarah, a smart little lass that you couldn't order or turn from what she wanted and she come with red hair and was aiming to be a cook or pastrymaker and dye her hair to do it, set face-forward she was for what she should be at eight years old, just turned, and her full brother Robert, a little dark clever lad with plumped cheeks and smelling always so fresh like a little apple, five-year-old, and then Annie Lovink's one, called Ann again, but getting Nancy, the same age, and if you could tell no other way, she was the brown-eyed one. And we all come on up over the bank and down among the watery ways and the reeds and rushes and all the running birds and a soft English wind and a steady sun and maybe a cloud chasing by, and the sea so far out you can't tell there is one. And myself a young chap not long gone thirty year old, for this was long ago. So see us, see us."

Arthur saw. He saw directly, with the children pictured in his mind, each one clearly there, even if the names he had heard were forgotten. He saw them moving in and out of the growing places on the marsh, where reeds tangled and fell, where low sandbanks had given a place where papery green plants grew direct from the grainy soil, where guttery waterways laced together and knotted and parted, where insects flew, great and small, where birds had let nests grow among the plants and wet weeds. He saw the children walk together into this place, staying with the man for a time and then finding new directions for themselves, things that each wanted to look at. The eldest boy was for finding the highest place and building it higher with the loose sand. The next boy helped for a time, but then chased the glamour of a huge fly as long as a hand and bright as silk, and flew after it turning his head from side to side, which was what the fly was doing as it hunted.

Two girls, one fair and the other auburn, were busy making a house, thatch first, because the reeds were easy to find and tie. Then they fell out in some way about it, and left in different directions; the fair one saying she would look at the sea, the auburn one that she would find something better, without knowing what it was. A little round boy and a girl with brown eyes (like Maureen Taski, he thought with a corner of his mind, until the corner began to crack its way into what he saw now, tearing him away from the marsh) played together, jumping a little creek and trying to catch frogs in the way that little children do, with their wrists rather than their fingers. The man leaned against a sandy bank and felt the sun on him, heard the voices of the children, and was next to sleep.

It was sleep, at last. To Arthur, sharing the experience, it was a sleep within a dream, when you know you sleep and know you will wake, perhaps at the beginning of the day just ended, perhaps in another world entirely. It was more like another day when he shared that waking. The sky had fallen grey and low, the wind had abandoned its light airs and was coming strongly off the land, whistling among the reeds and reefs and rippling the undercut waterways. The children were not in sight, large or small. Their voices could be heard calling in the distance, calling unknown and unhearable words. The man rose from his rest and called to them, and nothing came back that was certainly a reply. He called them name by name, and none of them came running in any fashion, tears or joy, laughing or crying. None of them came.

The man went from where he had been and looked for the children. He found in one place a digging on a sandbank, with the sand drying in the wind, and from that place tracks into the trackless. He found a bundle of tied reeds dropped in a path, and he came on the footprints of two children in some cold silt laid by a trickling drain, and the marks of their hands and the still free frogs. He came here and there on another footprint lying hidden in the deepening twilight, and he found the straw hat of the fair little girl, hung on a reed by its blue ribbon, full of wind.

Then he came on the sea, rising flat over this low land, ruled and silent and pressed by the wind, creeping unturnably. Along its margin he heard the voices of the children again, and knew the mastery of Thomas's tone, the startled eager cry of John, the question unanswered of Jane, Sarah's reproof to the day, and Robert and Nancy playing leap-frog, since they had caught nothing and had to do it themselves, with the bubbles and foam at the water's edge.

The man came back alone, wading through the salt water as it climbed higher. He took six children out that day, forgot them for a little while, and came again without them, getting up step by step on the sea wall and seeing the ocean spread below him, with nothing in it, nothing given back. The abominable marsh was covered, and with the marsh everything. At the last the man turned away and went inland, alone, and no voices followed him.

It was a bright hot afternoon in New Jersey. The sky was hazy, the wind gusty and hot. The old man leaned against his chair and was still. All that moved on him was a tear from the eye Arthur could see. It ran down his cheek and then back along his jaw. Arthur's own tears, which had come to him without a sob, ran down beside his nose and into his mouth.

"I'll take a turn on with you to . . to her house," said the old man.

"Yes," said Arthur, with the cold sea still chilling him when he stood up, and followed him. They walked straight across the sand, not bothering with the road. The dog followed. They came almost within seeing distance of the dog skeleton, but Arthur did not want to look. He was still expecting the sea to come over him, and what he had seen was more real than actual experience. But America returned to him as they walked, lightening his mind, so that when they joined the road again he was truly back in the present. The old man stopped, just as Arthur saw Aunt Deborah appear in her garden dressed, like a dragonfly, in shining blue-green silk, and walk up and down beside the front door. The old man, as if he had not seen, turned about and started home again. The dog saw and waited and let him pass before following again. Arthur went on. Aunt Deborah, like the strange children of the dream, had vanished too, but indoors, not in a marsh.

XIII

ARTHUR LOOKED back as he turned the corner to go to the back door, his usual way in. His grandfather was going slowly away, with the dog behind him, two small dark shapes against the bright expanse of sand. Above them, cutting from corner to corner of the sky, the railway bank was a tilted horizon. The other side of it, Arthur knew, there was sand, sea, the town; but part of him knew it was only the sea wall and the far side was all marsh, sweet or salt, down to the greedy tide.

He went in through the back door, wanting more peace for a little while. Perhaps he might be able to do something different from the rest of the day, like writing those postcards, or at least thinking of them, since they were still unbought. But there was no immediate peace.

In the kitchen Mother was standing in a heap of bright cloth. She was ankle-deep in it, and a cascade of it was coming from the table and deepening the heap she already had. She smiled in a flustered way when Arthur stood in the doorway, and gathered an armful of the stuff on the table. The rest of the table-full slid off and escaped her hand, which gathered at it absently with the wrist, as if she chased frogs.

"Oh," she said, "you're alone."

"Yes," said Arthur, wondering why she expected him to come in with Thomas and John, Jane and Sarah, little Robert and Nancy. For a moment he thought he was guilty of leaving them on the endless marshes.

"Deborah thought . . Aunt Deborah thought he, her father, might be coming here," said Mother.

"He just walked back with me," said Arthur. "He told me a sad story, and I listened like being there."

Mother put the handful of bright cloth remnants on the table again, and bent to scoop up more. "Then we needn't stop what we're doing," she said.

"Let's not do anything," said Arthur.

"We're in the middle of it," said Mother. "You'll see." Arthur sat down in the chair by the doorway and hoped that nothing was going to happen at all; that Mother and Aunt Deborah would put the cloth away and sit down too, quietly at the table, and read, while he clawed his way out of the stickiness joining today and some past time together, the feeling that pulled him apart and tied him together and made him uncomfortable now.

"Deborah," said Mother, calling through into the rest of the house. "You can come back as you are; he didn't come all the way."

"Oh mercy, all that trouble," said Aunt Deborah from beyond. "I just was beginning to think he hadn't after all."

She came through a moment later. She was dressed as Arthur had seen her, brightly in blue silk, with a red scarf tied round her head, and her eyes made large and young in some way. She had the guitar, with a yellow ribbon tied to its neck. She stood in the doorway like a statue for a second, and thrummed a chord on the strings.

"I gave up," she said. "I renounced Joseph and all his works and all his family."

"Now, don't get excitable," said Mother. "You just decided to go your own way, Deborah."

"Independence, freedom," said Aunt Deborah. "And his soul goes marching on. I will sing you a song, Arthur; I'm all ready to."

"It's quite all right, thank you," said Arthur, not wanting a song, or a word, or a note, or anything at all but to be left alone.

"You're welcome," said Aunt Deborah.

"Wait, girl," said Mother. "You are nothing like ready yet. You haven't a collar or a cuff, and that's no sort of a hat . . ."

"And I haven't a boy ready to help me," said Aunt Deborah. "Ready to help me and dressed the same."

"I'll get him ready in just a while," said Mother. "Now put that banjo down and hold still."

Arthur hoped he could watch and not be involved. Two people who were concentrating on each other would not be much disturbance to him, and he could sit facing in their direction as if he were watching and yet not watch at all.

But there was no escape. Mother was dressing Aunt Deborah up, and Aunt Deborah was going to dress him up. She called him two or three times, and he shook his head, until Mother told him not to be shy. He had to go and stand near the table and have cloth measured across his back and pinned to the shoulders of his shirt. He did not want to be touched and pawed and pressed and have to balance himself against the random tailoring movements of Aunt Deborah, who was being tailored in her turn. He preferred the times when a pin stuck into his skin; then there was a sharp pain as it went in, and a pull as it went out, but no bother about having to stand against it.

"Come on now," said Mother, after he had become very sulky and refused to turn round and be pinned down the front. "Join in," and she dumped a large prickly hat she had been making on to his head and he had to be angry or laugh, so he laughed and was ready to join in.

"You keep that hat," said Aunt Deborah. "It just makes you. Any old thing will do for me."

Aunt Deborah and Arthur were ready at last, and Mother was about to arrange them artistically and let the song begin when Aunt Deborah stopped her.

"Miriam," she said, "you need fine clothes just as much as we do."

"Oh no," said Mother; "I wouldn't look the same at all." But such words were no use against Aunt Deborah, and Mother began to get the treatment that Arthur had just finished having: pins and thumps and nudges, tightenings and stretchings, until she too was banded in colour from neck to the floor. Arthur took his turn at fabricating a hat and putting it on those greying curls.

"Now we can begin," said Aunt Deborah. "Get arranged, you all," and she prodded them into place.

"You're getting too excited, Deborah," said Mother.

"No," said Aunt Deborah. "It's been a long time without any fun; I'd forgotten what it was like. Now, squat down, Miriam, and bring your hand up here, like that, and you, Arthur, stand alongside. Now I expect we look fine. So I'll begin, and you can join the chorus when it comes round."

Then she played and sang the song called "Juanita".

> Soft o'er the fountain,
> Ling'ring falls the Southern moon

Far o'er the mountain
　　Breaks the day too soon!
　　In thy dark eyes' splendour,
Where the warm light loves to dwell,
　　Weary looks, yet tender,
　　Speak their fond farewell.
　　Nita! Juanita!
Ask thy soul if we should part!
　　Nita! Juanita!
　　Lean thou on my heart.

Arthur thought it was a silly song, and when it was repeated
for them all to join in he opened and closed his mouth and
hoped other people would make the sounds for him.

"No one can see us," said Aunt Deborah. "Now don't
either of you move." She left them to support her vanished
figure, and went to her bedroom for a mirror. She propped
it against the wall and they could all look into it and see part
of their group, posed against the kitchen table. Then they
sang another verse.

　　When in thy dreaming
Moons like these shall shine again,
　　And daylight beaming,
Prove thy dreams are in vain,
　　Wilt thou not, relenting,
For thine absent lover sigh?
　　In thy heart consenting
　　To a pray'r gone by?
　　Nita! Juanita!

Let me linger by thy side!
Nita! Juanita!
Be my own fair bride.

"No one can hear us," said Mother. But there is no equivalent to a mirror for sound except untrainable echo. Arthur wondered what to do about it. Aunt Deborah was ready to get up again and have the solution on her tongue, but it would not come to her in words.

It came instead in the form of the Preacher, darkening the kitchen door and tapping at it, so that all in the house stood still and listened, and then opening it and coming in beaming.

"Muz Thatcher, Muz Thatcher, bo-oy," he said. "I heard . . singing . . and I he-ard . . praises, like I never . . he-ard before, and I . . came in to Prai-ise the Lo-ord with my che-erful voice."

"Oh my," said Aunt Deborah, getting up and rushing out of the room into the yard past the Preacher. "I have my bowel complaint once more."

"Goodness, you haven't," said Mother, running out after her and holding her. Aunt Deborah turned and thumped Mother on the chest so that her next words were breathed out in a heap and wasted. Mother stopped and sat down on the ground, and laughed instead. The Preacher put out his great arm and lifted Aunt Deborah's right arm up into the air.

"This here is the winnah," he said, and grinned all round at an audience not there except in two places: Arthur by the kitchen table and Mother sitting in the yard outside.

Aunt Deborah pulled her arm away and thumped him on the chest with it.

"Don't strike . . me," rumbled the Preacher. "Girl. I am . . the Lo-ord's anointed."

Mother got up from the ground. "You can listen to us, Preacher," she said. "We just had the mirror listening and watching before." She and Aunt Deborah came in together. Arthur handed up the guitar, which had been left on the table.

"The merry harp . . with the lute," said the Preacher. "I guess your neighbour . . down the road . . your own . . father . . might well like to he-ar some music, Muz Thatcher, and it would che-er him to see you all coming from afar off, and say to himself, Who is this that cometh from Edom, with dyed garments from Bozrah? This that is glorious in his apparel, travelling in the greatness of his strength?"

"Shucks," said Aunt Deborah. "He doesn't care."

"I will go down with you, among the prophets," said the Preacher. Arthur noticed how some of his slow, full, words made the plates on the rack rattle and hum, as if his breath had been solid and touched them.

"We'll wait for the train to go by," said Aunt Deborah. "Then no one can see us."

The train passed us about five minutes later. During that time the Preacher stood expanding his smile just inside the kitchen door. Aunt Deborah attended busily to the tuning of her guitar, and Mother hid away some of the rough parts of Aunt Deborah's robe. Arthur lifted his warm head-dress a little way and then left it alone, because the pins in it had settled into his skull and movement scratched him, raising and lowering them. The Preacher said an occasional word of encouragement and the word roved round the room, too large to be absorbed by the walls immediately. Another thing the walls did not take in was the colour of the robes. The walls were wooden, and varnished, and the shine was now coloured like the cloth, with yellow blooming from one side of the fireplace, and red from the other, blue eclipsing the door to the rest of the house, and yellow showing through like the sun from the south wall. The other wall was darkened by the Preacher and lightened by door and window, so that nothing shone from it.

Then they went out, and drew sound and colour with them, leaving the mirror to look at nothing. Arthur wanted to stay, to see what it was like and how long the robes stained the memory of the wall. He wanted to stay behind for another reason too, so that he was not part of the intrusion by strangers on his own grandfather. Of course, Aunt Deborah and Mother belonged as much as he did, but it was to him that the old man talked, and it was to him that he handed on sight of things that had perhaps not ever happened. The man from the sea, for instance, he had almost witnessed with some inner eye, and certainly the old man had not seen him either. And today's story of the marsh had been shared in the same way, springing up from a memory they both shared but neither had experienced as an event.

They walked down the road. Arthur wondered how the sand was taking up the colours of the cloth, and how much the sky reflected it.

"I'm too warm," said Aunt Deborah. "I'm running like a candle."

They went on. The dog saw them first, and stood up, wondering where to bite in the fence of brightness that hid all legs but the Preacher's. The old man sat still in his chair and looked at each face in turn to find who it was.

"We come to bring you Joy . . . and Song," said the Preacher.

"You didn't bring tea this time again, then Deborah?" said the old man.

"Just singing, Pa," said Aunt Deborah, in a not-very-boisterous voice. "Singing."

"I've heard you many a time," said the old man. "I don't forget things."

Aunt Deborah plucked three solitary notes with her left thumb, and they fell melancholy into the sand.

"Now," said the Preacher, "something bright to end the day, what about it Muz Thatcher, Muz Thatcher, Praise the Lo-ord at the going-down of the same . . ."

"Songs," said the old man. "What I would like is what we had at the chapel the time Edith was buried, long ago, when we'd waited day after day to see who was to be laid by. Scarlet fever come to Osney Cold Fen, and there was one child swelled with it and then another, Jane and John, Thomas and Robert, Sarah, that was all in three days laid dead, and then Peter that was born on the fourth day and whether he was baptized live or dead only God knows, and after Peter went his mother, Edith. And the opposite neighbour, young Mrs Lovink, Annie, or Nancy, but not the little one. They all went together, that was mine, in the chapel yard at Cold Fen, and there was Martha laid there in Osney church at an Epiphany, and the rest round Trinity Sunday, and I don't forget nothing, yet for all that I'd like to hear the funeral hymn once more, for the next time I'll not listen myself, loud as it is."

"Pa," said Aunt Deborah, "you needn't think of going."

"Depends how I like the tune," said the old man. "'Tis one of the old ones, 'When on my day of life.'"

The Preacher hummed a tune. It was like a cart going over a bridge.

"It's a sad, long, fine one," said Aunt Deborah, fingering out a chord, and stroking a tune. She sang:

"When on my day of life the night is falling,
And in the winds from unsunned spaces blown
I hear far voices out of darkness calling
My feet to paths unknown."

She paused, and began another verse. "You might know this," she said. "Miriam." But it was the old man who joined the next lines, in a new young voice that startled them all:

"Some humble door among thy many mansions,
Some sheltering shade where sin and striving cease;
And flows for ever through heaven's green expansions,
The river of thy peace."

And then he held up his hand to stop the singing, got up from his chair, and went indoors, and left them.

"We'll go home now," said Aunt Deborah. "We never make each other happy."

XIV

By the time they got home, Aunt Deborah was in one of the worst tempers Arthur had seen on anybody; nearly as bad, he thought, as one of Maureen Taski's throwing-screaming-and-biting furies.

Aunt Deborah had begun to mutter when they were half way across the sand on the way home. She had pulled her hat off and let it fall to pieces. Arthur had picked up the tawdry rags it broke into.

"What we look like I don't know," she said. "But I never felt so ridiculous. And what we did down there, singing that old melancholy hymn, I don't know."

"John Greenleaf Whittier was a great man," said Mother. " 'Be near me when all else is from me drifting . . .' That's famous, Deborah; and you know he was for freedom."

"And that Preacher," said Aunt Deborah, tearing off her collar and taking no notice of Mother's words. Arthur picked up the collar. "That Preacher coming in my house like that. It'll be all over town, and they'll hear of it, Joseph's people, how we went out crazily at night."

"We haven't had supper yet by a long way," said Mother.

"Supper indeed," said Aunt Deborah. "That's over for the day, Miriam. You've had your last meal in my house. You can be out before breakfast in the morning; you've been here long enough to turn me silly, and you can go satisfied. There isn't anyone that cares now, no, not anyone. *He* never cared, back there, never. He only cared for his black-eyed Susan in England, not for any of his own."

"Nancy," said Arthur, before Mother could stop the word.

"Don't say that name," said Aunt Deborah, pulling off her sleeves and stamping them into the road. "I won't hear it." She began to tear at the bodice of the costume she wore, but it was all too firmly pinned to what was underneath and would not come away.

"I can't get it off," she said. "There isn't anything right." To make up for it she trampled the hem off her skirt, in the gateway of the house, and went on Cinderella'd in tatters. Arthur and Mother picked up the torn pieces and followed her in.

"Don't you say another word," said Mother. "She got so excited before that it was bound to end in tears, like a birthday party."

"At a party you get something to eat," said Arthur. "Do we get anything today?"

"Oh hush," said Mother. "You make me laugh, and we mustn't. I just hope she didn't lock us out because I don't want to go up into Arnott's Bay dressed like this, if we have to leave tonight."

The back door was open. They went in. Aunt Deborah had swept through the kitchen, tearing off more pieces as she went, and was in her bedroom now, tugging and ripping and talking crossly to the pins.

"We're in," said Mother, stepping over the threshold. "Now let's get dressed in our right minds and have supper."

They had supper, and tidied up the kitchen, lit the lamp,

and sat talking by the dying stove. It was very pleasant, they thought, and something they had not been able to do for a long time, just sit and do nothing comfortably, undisturbed. In the next room Aunt Deborah slept gently. At last Mother put out the kitchen lamp, lit the candle, and took Arthur and herself off to bed. They sat on the edges of their beds and plucked silk and pins from the folds of their garments.

In the morning Aunt Deborah was cheerful again. There was no talk of leaving by the first train. In fact, it had gone before she called them. There was no guitar music, though sometimes Arthur thought he heard words in the air, about far voices out of darkness calling, or rivers flowing for ever through heaven's green expansions, quite without any sadness or anger.

During the morning Arthur and Mother went to Arnott's Bay. This time, by thinking about it from the moment of leaving the kitchen door, and by tying knots in Mother's belt, and putting a pebble in his shoe, the postcards were remembered and actually chosen. By now Arthur had forgotten any good reason for sending one to Maureen Taski, who was nothing to him, with her tantrums and her temper and her creepiness. He knew he had to buy two cards, and he did. One could go to Lorna that very day, he decided, and the second could go in about a week's time. He put the cards beside his bed, when he got back, to write them that night, without fail. To make sure of it he bought stamps and stamped them, which was half the job done. The rest of the day he could spend thinking of something that had happened that was small enough to mention. The pictures on the cards were of the shore town where they had gone one day, and a New Jersey fishing boat with some of New Jersey looking grey behind it.

The old man had come out of his kitchen again, when

Arthur went that way in the afternoon. Arthur settled down in his usual place and waited to hear what there was to hear.

"That girl is getting more than I thought," he said. "There wasn't nothing like that in Osney in my day, except some Christmas times there was a day when the mummers come round and demonstrated their play. But that was a laughable play, in parts, and 'twould never do here, being about England and Saint George, coming in and killing the dragon, like it might have happened. Well, we never did hit it off right; she come out different from what I expected, and that's it, is that. I daresay she took affront yesterday when I closed the door on her. I was just going for the words to that hymn, to let all sing clearer, and I wasn't having her march in after me, and she knowed it, and she stalked off with all. Aye, she was raised simple, but she bred out proud, and I don't know how, for her mother and me, we couldn't be less than we were, not any ways."

"She was mad when she got home," said Arthur.

"Ah," said the old man. "I been mad too, that way. I been a dotterel, and I been raving with rages." He looked back over his old rages and the ways he had been against the world. He lit his pipe again, and puffed at it.

"They near put me away after that scarlet fever," he said. "I was brought to nothing, though it never touched me. That can't be seen, any more than the marsh-drench can be, but the marsh-drench don't kill so sudden, nor so many, and it don't trouble little ones so hard, maybe it makes them lazy-daisy betimes, but it don't bring them down with a great pain in the head, and then leave them lifeless. A man can fight the tide, he can fight the fire, he can fight famine, but not what he can't see, and that frightens most. And I raged most against it, until they would have taken me off to the mad-house. Well, I didn't want that, so I went off again to Loddenham and took my own fever cure, all that summer long, and laid in my bed in the house and gazed on the wall by day, and walked abroad at night, out of folks' way. I couldn't bear to be looked on and pitied.

"There was a night of winter, when the snow drove in and hid those new graves, and I was so tied in my dreams then I thought they had gone for ever and a new world was born without a mark ready to live on. But 'twas only snow, running wet underneath, chilling all. Then the moon came out and all was bright, and the wind whipping and driving the snow."

Arthur could feel this snow, related closely to sand, covering and uncovering an unknown countryside, not the countryside of the hymn, and heaven's green expansions, but Osney and Osney Cold Fen. Osney Cold Fen was behind him, and the wind was out of the east, burning and biting in its coldness.

The snow did not lie everywhere. The new fields round Osney Cold Fen were standing with water. Some were completely under it, and others had it running like the teeth of long combs along furrows. As the snow came and went the moonlight showed the water as dark against snowy ground, or light against dark earth.

There was a rising in the waters, and the low fields were more and more covered with water, coming slowly from the far river, seeping over banks that were not high enough. It flowed so slowly that the snows of the ridges of the fields were lifted undisturbed and lay on the water as if on solid land, and slowly curved under the current, so that it looked as if the land were bending.

After a long watching all the fields were covered, and the

water was knee deep in the road. Arthur was aware of being the watcher in the road and of not being wetted by the water. Then he saw from the sea wall, where the marsh lay beyond. The marsh was covered by a tide, as he had seen it before. But this tide was more and more, and was not lying full and still, but coming up the wall against the sleeping land. There was no snow falling now, and from this sea came no drifting flakes, because all that had fallen there had melted and gone. Something like snow came, but it was broken water, as white but not so cold.

He could see far round. He could see further than one man at one time; down to the great river to the south, and beyond it, all one sheet of water, calm inland, with bridges and trees standing on their own crisp shadows, black and white on silver, and the course of the river marked by posts alone. There was a glow of lanterns, red and yellow, on the big bridge, and out where the sea touched the land there was the bank of the sea wall, a narrow dark line still above water.

Northwards it was the same, except that here some of the wall had broken, with water either side, and the sea was coming in, swirling and moving the thick flood beyond. And now there was nowhere any snow to blow, there was nothing to check the sight, from here in the midst of the waters at the sea's edge, to the low hills inland.

The sea lifted slowly over the bank, all the way along. But Arthur, in his watching, was not wetted by it any more than he had been by the inland waters. He moved with it, down below it, and walked in some dream fashion along the road with the waters overhead gathering the moonlight, and the waves of incoming sea passing through the moonlight like the ridge and furrow of the ploughland.

A boat went by overhead, and either side of it two oar-blades dipped black and almost unrelated, and there were voices from above, and it seemed there was sunshine up there, and that day had come.

Great fish came swimming by, and that was not unnatural. But less expected was a greyhound, and then another one, running about among the drowned hedgerows. The underwater place changed to the churchyard, and the church stood half under water, with the great fish swimming in and out of the green windows in the aquarium silence, and the dogs were in the church now, looking out, and watching the fish over their heads.

The church doors were open, and there was a whale inside, occupying all the middle of the church, with its head by the altar and its tail under the tower, lying there, watching for some resurrection.

The spiral stair in the tower led up out of the water, and the stone was a different colour above, in the air, in the cold daylight, and there was frost setting the water against the stone, thickening it as it lapped, so that the church was ringed with an extra course of new-laid clear stone.

Outside there was water stretching to the end of the world, full of silence, waiting for the great ebb of time to take it away. And the dogs ran about under the water, and under it there seemed to be all the old life going on as it once had in unsunned spaces, but only going on while the water stood. When the water went all below it would cease until the next time.

But it was New Jersey, and a hot summery day, dry, with a dry sky, and the wall of the house so arid that no water could ever have been there at all. The old man was sitting there peacefully, thinking back to old times perhaps, but not having any thoughts now that Arthur could share. For him that tide had gone out again, and maybe would not come again.

"Tides are moving in the water," said the old man. "I often think of that. But time must be a moving in something, but what I don't know. That what I just tell you of, I don't reckon ever was, so maybe it has yet to come, part and part of it. Tides come again, and so do times, and that time after I lost them all I don't want no more. 'Twas too cruel for mortals, and too kind as well. I had what I could live on, and no need of want, but 'twas all tasteless to me, and there was nothing of it I wanted, not even feeling my hunger and thirst, only for the Indian flowers. So it came about that I made hay by moonlight, the saying is, and never had it cut till it was rotting, and never laid knife to the wheat, and left the potatoes to be their own seed, until there was nothing left, and then I came to want and hunger and cold; all, all, was wasted away. And at the last I had to leave, but that's another time, another tide, when I tell you that."

Arthur got up to go. He had stayed longer than he thought. Far down the railway line he heard the train coming, like a tide about to overtop the bank between him and the sea. That thought was drowned in the next one, that there was generally something to eat at about the time the train passed the house. Yesterday had been different. He ran home, wondering, some of the time, whether he might be under water, and whether two greyhounds might spring along beside him, moving curiously in and out of the air.

Aunt Deborah, having started a new and unpredictable patch of life by playing the guitar again, had gone a stage further in wickedness, she said, and had played cards all the afternoon with Mother. After their meal they sat round the table and played again. Then there was something even more unJoseph-like, when she offered to tell fortunes with the cards.

"No," said Mother. "I'm not superstitious. I don't believe in that kind of thing; it's unlucky."

"Well, that doesn't make sense," said Aunt Deborah. "I'll do Arthur's."

Arthur's fortune was to travel. Aunt Deborah thought it must be by train, because there was no ship in the fortune. She reckoned he was going to Mexico, because he would have to stay in America.

"I shall fly," said Arthur. But the cards had never heard of that. They had heard, though, that he would find his sweetheart abroad. Arthur was not interested in that, but it reminded him to go to bed and write his postcards. However, while he still wondered what to say in the space provided, Mother came to bed too, and had the candle out before he had composed the few words needed. He gazed at the card in the dark, dropped it on the floor, and went to sleep, knowing he would have the right words as soon as he woke in the morning.

XV

ARTHUR WOKE in the morning, and his private promise to the night before was fulfilled: he had thought of something wise and witty and short for one of the postcards, all ready to write down. It was an early waking, and not quite broad day. He sat up, found the card he had dropped and discovered it had the wrong picture, because the message he had thought of did not fit the town scene. The other card, with the fishing boat on, was not right either. When he woke he knew that the one with aeroplanes on was the right one, but now he had moved about he woke further still and found he had imagined part of the solution. But the fishing boats would have to do, and he still knew there was a brilliant thing to be said. He took the pencil Aunt Deborah had found for him, and wrote 'Dear Lorna', on the card.

Nothing happened. The pencil left no mark at all. It slid about on the shiny paper and there was no silvery black trail. Three times Arthur tried to write 'Dear Lorna', and three times nothing was left. But he knew he was awake. Awake enough to go to the window and draw the curtain right back and let in all the light there was. That had no effect on the pencil mark, but it did show up a sort of valley he had made in the paper by pressing hard. He looked carefully at the pencil, and found it was real, though not very sharp. Then he gave up the struggle with it and got back into bed, and tried to memorise the message that was in his mind.

That too had been written with a dead pencil. He could not get it into his mind at all clearly. At last he went to sleep with it, and woke without it, when Aunt Deborah rattled at the door.

"It's a very hard pencil," said Mother, when they were both up. Aunt Deborah said it was one from Arnott's Bay City Bank and had to be hard to write through the copy paper. After breakfast she got out a pen and a bottle of ink, and Arthur tried with that. It was not much better. The ink rolled up into little balls and gathered at the end of the strokes of the nib, or in the little valleys the pencil had dug. The postcard was too shiny for any sort of writing. Aunt Deborah took the ink away, in case of splashes, and blotted the card. It came out dry and unmarked, except for some fingerprints that were beginning to make both sides grimy.

"She doesn't want a card," said Arthur. "That's four times I've tried to write her name and it won't work, and I can't remember what I was going to say."

The cards were left for that day, and for a day or two more. One day there was a return visit from the people they had visited in the town. Before they came Aunt Deborah had gone back into her quiet mood and darker clothes, and spent a whole day polishing and cleaning. On the day Arthur had had to look after the little boy, who had climbed on the yard fence and pulled a length of it down, made dirty marks on two of the house windows, made the privy seat damp probably on purpose, and made Arthur walk backwards into a stack of flowerpots, breaking eight of them. Arthur felt he was to blame for all those things. In the house the little boy dropped a plate, spilled something unknown but sticky on a red velvet cushion, kicked up a corner of the parlour oilcloth, found the playing cards where they had been hidden and spread them all out (but Mother tidied them away before the rest of his family saw them), and at last hit his head on the corner of the kitchen cupboard so that he bled on the wall and made a mark for ever.

"There," said Mother, when they had gone, "are you Josephed enough now, Deborah?"

"They're my friends," said Aunt Deborah. "You're going away next week so it's easy for you to pick and choose, you're away from home. I know I can do what I like, but only out of so many things; there isn't all the world to choose from. I can't choose to wear my diamonds tonight and the pearls to-morrow; I can't choose to go to tea with the Governor of the State; I can't even choose to have new friends or go visiting my own brother, because I have my own Pa to look after, and it isn't even any use visiting him: he don't care at all. There isn't all the choice in the world, Miriam. I've got Joseph's family, whether I like or not, and it's no use pretending they won't always be there, just the other side of Arnott's Bay, knowing the same folk I know and telling the same tales I tell, and coming here to find me the same as I was last time, and the time before."

Mother said it was all true, but Deborah, you mustn't grow into an old maid. "If I can't tell you, who can?" And, said Mother, it was to be hoped that the little boy was not always going to be as he was today.

"I can't choose to tell him to keep away," said Aunt Deborah.

Arthur had not thought much about when they were to

leave. For a day or so after hearing it was 'next week' he went about thinking there would be seven days more. But when he asked, and Mother and Aunt Deborah got down to counting on fingers and calendars, he found three more days and nights were in hand, and then it was a question of the first train in the morning, and the visit would be over. Then he began to feel the memories of home tugging at him, and he wanted to be there at once, for the journey to exist that took him home, but not have to be lived through in all its length.

He went down the road to his grandfather, to say that he would be going soon. The old man took his hand for a moment, in a long handshake of an unmoving sort.

"I never said Goodbye to anyone," he said. "I don't reckon to start now. All that went from me went without farewell, and I left them the same way. I'm not one that holds on things, and I'm not one that folk hold on to. I ain't ever been prickly enough to cling, nor yet smooth enough to grasp, which is the same as most folk. I'm just a pebble that never got weathered through. There was a time I thought to be a diamond, glittering like Parson Ramage, but it isn't so; I'm just hard mud, not quite rock, not quite sand. There's some footprints on me, trod deep, but most things smoothed me away. Well, however long we both stay, I shan't get most things told. Some things I've said, the best I can, and all real to me, though not all real to others. There ain't no more to know about me."

Arthur thought there was one thing he did not know, and that was what kind of bird a dotterel was.

"Very inconsiderable and foolish," said the old man. "One of the plover sort, and simple-minded. They make a good figure of me, for see how the world takes me every time. Whatever I do I find the world did it first, and I didn't choose, I just threw the net over my own head. But I don't complain of what befell me, no, not at all. I might just argue I always think the wrong way round, that's all, and wanted more than there is. I wanted to be struck in with the world, but it wouldn't join me. We all were spoilt down there in the marshes, tasting ourselves stupid with Indian flowers and dreaming. There was three times I came to nothing, no roof over me, no cash to hand, no anything, just a hollow sickness, like getting the feathers to eat instead of the bird. So there I was, in Osney Cold Fen, and nothing to my name but an illness worse than fever, and 'twas reckoned I was to die, soon. So I reckoned I might as well drown as wait, and set off south to the river to sit by the bank until the high tide, or perhaps a boat would come and take me to Wisbech again. Well, there come a boat, and I heaved stuff on it, I don't rightly know what, barley or bricks, or hay or horses, I don't know. We had one thing and another. But we came at last to another place like Wisbech, but 'twas over in Low Germany, where the Dutch ships come from. And so it came about that I was on a Dutch ship, with all these Dutchies, bound for here, and lying low with one death as good as another, I couldn't tell what I was dying of. But when I came to be myself and still alive, and looked out on deck when my turn come, there was the sea for ever, sun up and sun down, and so for days and weeks, until we come in under a town and landed off to an island, and they shouted at us in Dutch and let us into the land bit by bit. All the Dutchies, they rushed off west, away from the sea, but I stayed by it, and came down here, walking for a few days, and getting market-garden work, like I've done plenty of at home. And then I steeled down a bit, and came on Florence, that was next thing to Annie Lovink in looks, and there was Clifford and Deborah. And there ain't a fever in me now, and no new dreams, only the old ones wearing thinner, and coming further away."

There was silence from the old man. He let his pipe lie cold in his hand. It was the last silence that he and Arthur had between them, privately. It was the time when Arthur was joining himself to the end of the old man's story, when he was joining himself to past time and growing his own history. He found that since being in New Jersey he had become older than anyone and any place he knew. At the end of the last silence the old man said his age. Arthur realized that his grandfather was older than the town at home, older than the railway, older than the State he lived in, which had been a Territory then, or perhaps not even discovered.

But it was time to leave for dinner. "I guess I have to go now," said Arthur. He held out his hand, in the politest gesture he knew. "It's been a great pleasure meeting you, Sir," he said.

The old man stood up, startled by this act, and managed to shake hands. The dog, not knowing what was happening, got up as far as it could in the time there was, and bit Arthur's ankle. It tickled. He pulled the leg out of the dog's mouth, and went away laughing. The old man stood and watched him go, saying: "I ain't called Sir, I ain't called Sir," but he was not displeased at all.

Mother was doing the beginning of packing, and debating with Aunt Deborah about whether to pack some things dirty or clean. No one was sure whether the next day, which was the last full day, would be dry enough to hang clothes out. In the end some clothes were packed dirty.

That evening Aunt Deborah sat about rather primly for some time, and then made an effort and overcame the primness. She got out the guitar and tried a song. But there were two things wrong. One was that she was trying to jolly along an evening that ought to go slowly, since it was the last but one, and the other was that she had really decided that the guitar was not something she should indulge in. When she had torn the bright costume from herself a few days before she had at the same time surely given up for ever the wilder excitements of her young days. She said so in the end, putting the guitar in its case. "I'm to be an old maid," she said. "I'm not sorry, and I'm not unhappy. Arthur, it won't be worth visiting me again until you're a grown man and I'm quite old. I'll be quite happy if I stay as I am, but I'll have to stay with the folk I know, up in Arnott's Bay, and we'll visit each other, them and me, until we forget we're people at all, and we're just like furniture that time is dusting."

Then she took the pack of fortune-telling cards and dropped them on the back of the fire. "I don't want to know the future," she said. "It's clear to me already. Miriam, I'm right glad you came, and I'm right glad you tried to pull me out of my settled ways. But I'm going back into them, and I won't worry about changing any more. I'm going to be as happy as I am. And Arthur, it's been a pleasure to have you here, and as good to me as rearing my own child, and I'm real happy with all your visit, both of you."

They both said they had been real happy too. Arthur repeated his speech of the morning, but saying Ma'am instead of Sir, and Aunt Deborah kissed him.

Then they all went to bed.

"Those postcards," said Arthur, because they were still lying on the bedside table.

"I'll get you a pencil in the morning," said Mother. "You can write them both then."

Arthur remembered then how he had meant to send one to Maureen Taski in the hope of stopping her from becoming a neglected creep and an old maid. But his feelings about Aunt Deborah had changed with time. At first he had not liked her fussed ways, and wanted to preserve others from being like her. But he had seen that change was not always the desired thing, and he had seen that Aunt Deborah was a person, like anyone he knew, able to sulk and shout and laugh and make improper remarks and have a bowel complaint, even if it was imaginary. In the end she had chosen to be what she wanted to be. She said it was because there was no choice, but there was a choice, and she had made it. If she had gone on to be a gay singing person again she would have found different friends. As it was, she had chosen the old ones. He asked Mother a question he had in mind for some time, but hadn't felt it was his business to know. He still thought it might not be, and that he could be told to keep out of things that did not concern him. He had often heard of things that were nothing to do with him.

"Who is Joseph?" he said.

"I thought you knew," said Mother. "Well, a lot of what went on can't have meant much to you. Joseph was going to marry Aunt Deborah a long time ago, but he was killed in the war, not even fighting but in the camp in South Carolina. So they never got married, but he left her this house and money, and she has that to live on. That nasty little boy is Joseph's nephew, and I think she's lucky, she might have had one like it herself. I think Joseph was different from them, but he might have been going to be the same. That was when she stopped playing the guitar and being a wild young thing, or as wild as you can get in Arnott's Bay. Joseph would have been your uncle. He had a hardware shop with his brother, and sold buckets and mops and galvanized hen-coops and nails and roof-stuff. He built this house with his own hands, all those nails he drove in, every one. It's down here, unfashionable, because of your grandfather. Deborah wanted to keep an eye on him, you know, not too far away."

"He won't stay still," said Arthur, remembering another thing he wanted to know but would probably not find out now: who lived in which house down there on the sands? Which was the middle one of them, church, or ruin, or the old man? He fell asleep as he tried to invent a method of doing it without fail.

Mother blew out the candle and its smoke drifted about in the darkness.

XVI

ARTHUR GOT the postcards written during the morning. They were both to Lorna Rackham. The first one said:

"Dear Lorna,

"I am at the ocean. My grandfather lives here. Also my aunt, but not together. We went to this place one day and had chicken, it was fried east coast style, sincerely Arthur."

That was the one with the shore town on.

The one with the boat said:

"Dear Lorna, I have been near a boat like this" ("I didn't know that," said Mother. "When?") but not on the ocean. We mended some nets with a preacher. I will go abroad later on my aunt says, and hope to see you soon, sincerely, Arthur."

"They're ridiculously bad to write on," said Mother, taking the cards and blowing away some soft pencil dust. "Now we have to post them."

"Not all at once," said Arthur. "One today, one tomorrow."

"Yes," said Mother. "Must keep the interest going, I suppose."

During that morning they did another layer of packing, so

that there would be hardly any to do early the next day. It was mostly wrapping shoes in newspaper, which was interesting to do the first time because shoes generally lie about in hallways or under beds or on feet near the ground out of the way, rather than being hidden in bundles one at a time.

"I don't know how we got all this in when we came," said Mother. "Have you been buying clothes?"

In the afternoon Mother and Arthur went down the road to say goodbye to his grandfather. Aunt Deborah said she would leave herself behind this time, since she could go down there any time with no trouble, and they didn't want sharp words today. "Sometimes he doesn't speak at all," she said. "Like someone special."

Arthur thought it unnecessary for him to go, too, but probably right for him to be there if Mother was. He had already got used to the idea that he had seen the old man for the last time, that there was nothing more to say.

There was not much for Mother to say, either. They had come to New Jersey so that she could talk with Deborah, and Arthur with the old man, as well as for the change. Now she stood on the stoop and thanked him for talking to her son, and Arthur stood by like no one who belonged to this place.

"I've liked to talk to him, Miriam," said the old man. "We fared well together. My own children never heard what he has heard. When they would have listened it was all too near, and now they don't want to hear. An old man should have grandchildren to tell tales to, and if he can't make them up then they must be true ones. And now I'll walk back with you some part of the road."

He came back with them halfway along the road, and then stopped. "I'll watch you the rest of the way," he said. "Don't be looking back. I've a short time to remember you, so I must see all I can. You have a long time to remember me if you want to, so don't waste it looking at what there isn't much of."

"Well, I don't like to go marching off like that," said Mother. "Isn't there something we can do more for you?"

"Yes," said the old man. "Bury me here somewhere, I care little for that; but go to Osney Cold Fen and mark out where Edith is, and all the little ones, and where Annie lies, if no one did that."

"Yes," said Arthur.

"Stones, put up stones," said the old man. "But nothing like gentlefolk, just humble."

"I will," said Arthur. "I know."

"Trinity Sunday, 1886," said the old man. "When 'twas. Now go, the pair of you."

They obediently turned away and left him standing and watching them. Arthur was glad he had come this extra time after the last, to have this duty put on him of remembering for the rest of the world that distant day in a distant chapel yard.

"I shall go there one day," he said. "I know all about them, all his children."

"They are my brothers and sisters-in-law," said Mother. "I do not know who they were."

"I will tell you," said Arthur, and as they walked along he gave each one a name, and a description.

"I think that's enough," said Mother. "You won't forget, I know, but I don't want to know more now. This is meant to be holiday."

"I'll go and get the postcards and mail them," said Arthur.

But when they came into the house they found it impossible

to go out again. While they had been gone Aunt Deborah had made up a party meal for them. She had watched them come up the road, and everything was hotly ready for them to sit down to it.

"This is like old times," she said. "I've been hiding and hiding and laying things in for days, and as soon as you went out I scampered to town and brought everything down, and here it is. I just thought for a moment Pa was coming with you, so I made it ready. He turned back, I guess."

"He just saw us on a piece," said Mother.

"Wouldn't have come, I daresay" said Aunt Deborah. "But I made some English tea for him. I'll take him down a box in the morning; I feel ashamed of not doing it before in a long time, but he pecks like a little bird and that old dog gets the most of it all."

The feast lasted several hours, ebbing and flowing, sometimes dying away to a lamplit heap of dirty plates and then waking again to a dish of something new that came ready in the oven. Arthur finished before the meal did, by falling asleep at the table and going to bed not quite awake as the great dish-washing began. He was so sleepy that he took his shoes off, wrapped them in his shirt, and put it in the wicker box that was standing on Mother's bed.

In the morning he could remember nothing about it, but he must have done it, because there was no shirt to be found, and no shoes. Mother had fastened up the wicker box, but she undid it again and looked in, and found the missing articles. Arthur put them on, still half asleep: last night and this early morning were much the same thing to him.

No one wanted any breakfast. Aunt Deborah said she would come all the way to Philadelphia with them, because she hadn't been in a long time. They all went out of the house together, bundled up with more packets and bags than they had brought, Arthur was sure. The train came in at four minutes to eight, and they got on it.

"At least," said Aunt Deborah, "we can say goodbye when we're awake, instead of now. I'd hate to go back in the house now and pull your warm beds to pieces and not have you coming in and out."

For the beginning of the journey Arthur looked from the window. He saw Aunt Deborah's house get smaller and lose itself. He saw the bowl of sand with the three houses in the middle, and realized that he still did not know which was which from a distance. Then they too had dropped back and out of sight behind trees, and the train was running along the line that went forever homewards.

The city, where they had to change trains, was hot, noisy, and smelt of overcooked food and smoke. Mother waited for the platforms of the station to stop whirling, and then asked the way to the next train. There was less time than they thought, and they hurried on their way.

"It's going to be a quick goodbye after all," said Aunt Deborah.

"We've got someone else's bags as well as ours," said Mother. "I think you must have done that, Deborah."

"We're about right," said Aunt Deborah. "I'd been meaning to give you a final tune before you went, and then go right out and sell the guitar. But there's no time for a tune, and it seems to me Arthur might need something like a guitar one of these days, so here you are, boy."

She put one of the bundles into his arms as he stood on the step of the train.

"That's pleased you," she said. "Oh shucks, your train's going out now, and I never had time to say a thing, Miriam. Give my love to Clifford, tell him his Pa's all right, far as I can make out, well, you've seen him, you'll find how to tune that instrument, Arthur, I put the book in, it's an old fashioned book but it's an old guitar." Now she was being left behind, and was standing on tip toes and waving and shouting about coming again and enjoying having them and have a good journey, and then the doors were firmly closed against the passengers, and they settled to the long voyage, of four hours or more up the mountains and a long wait high in the shrill air of the mountain town before a cold night of slow going down the other side into a different air.

After the long night there was the long day through the plain. It had changed now from what it was, with more ripeness in everything, a different set of colours lying in the fields. But there was the same effect of uniformity over it all, the same model houses and doll people and toy trucks, artificial trees. Arthur had a sleepy afternoon theory that they might really be in a long tunnel and the landscape painted on its wall, to help the journey along.

Then, late in the afternoon but still before evening, the train stopped for them, and they got out. Dad was there, and not saying anything, but opening the door of the big truck and letting Mother in and throwing the baggage in the back and moving off at once. It was the only way to stop Mother being ill for certain. They rushed on for a while, and then slowed down, and came to a walking pace. Mother nodded, Dad stopped the truck, and they were all able to say hello without illness.

"Right now, home," said Mother. "I've just been missing

it and missing it the last two weeks; there's always so much to do there."

"Me and home have been missing you," said Dad.

"Dad," said Arthur, who had been looking in his pocket as a certain thing became more and more certain to him. "Will you stop at the corner. I just have to mail some cards I forgot to send before I left." And two cards to Lorna Rackham went into a box about a hundred yards from where she lived. "I didn't actually forget her," he said.

XVII

THE JOURNEY lasted all night and all day. Even before the night had closed against the transparency of the dome Art had seen for long enough the narrow horizon of the sea running along the edge of the sky. There had been no change in it for hours. When the daylight deepened into blue twilight and then swooped into blackness he was glad to be able to stop searching distance and wait for what he was looking for to come to him.

Nothing came out of the night. The engines of the B17 Flying Fortress tore invisible holes in the night and brought the bomber to a bleak, high, chill field in Iceland. There was an Arctic silence when the engines stopped. Human voices were like the yelping of foxes along the wind, and the cracking of the cooling engines like bubbles bursting on a glass of Coke. For a little while this was a foreign country, and then it was part of the 8th Air Force again, in the buildings and the routine. Only, in the morning, strange mountains stood round the airfield.

In the morning the journey began again. Art, buttoned and zipped and padded into his flying suit, was high in his dome long before take-off, and could see the northern mountains and the northern sea and a low horizon.

"How do we go on?" he asked the tail gunner.

"Nobody told me geography this far east," said the tail gunner. "I guess it's ocean all the way to England."

The mountains sank down below the horizon and were no more. Far to the north a white mist or lying snow glowed red in the morning, then blue, then white. Before it could change again it was beyond sight. Below and all round was the Atlantic, empty, and above there was a clear sky. The day went on without variety. The engines dragged them along in thunder and seemed to get them nowhere. Another B17, two miles away, hung unmoving in one sector of Art's dome, keeping station as if the two bombers were joined by a girder, or one was a reflection of the other.

The sea below stayed empty, uninhabited. Here and there, as the day went by, there was a patch of a different colour, where a cloud stood on its shadow. The darker places grew more common and were at last filling the gentle distances. He watched for them to join up into a greater solidity and become a headland, or a beach, or an island. But the water would not lift itself into rock.

Then his landscape watching stopped. He saw below, and running at a cross course, his first warplane of a foreign air force. It was a British flying boat, skimming the waves in a lower layer of air, bound on quite other foreigner's business. Art remembered that he was a quarter English, a fact that had made the tail gunner laugh when Art mentioned it before they left the States. Art sure looked it, he said.

The clouds closed in more on them. The accompanying B17 began to slide away from station now and then, as moving air took one or other of the bombers and slid it to one side or up or down. Art began to think of other things with part of his mind. He found it best to do that in bumpy conditions.

The day before he had been in Nova Scotia. Three days before that he had been at McGuire Air Force Base in New Jersey, with nothing to do for a day. He had borrowed a car and driven across the State to Arnott's Bay, coming slowly towards the town through the pinewoods. He had been disappointed by the town. Those years before, ten or eleven now, when he had stayed several weeks in the district, it had seemed real and solid. Now it was composed of elderly shacks, and the shops were small and dirty, the streets raw gravel. The house where Joseph's kin lived was shuttered tight against the late summer winds. But in any case he had not wanted to pause there. He had driven to the station and crossed the track and gone down a few yards—which had been a long slope down a lane last time—and come to a little wooden house retired in green bushes.

He had stopped the car and left it blocking the lane. There seemed to be no road beyond, in any case. He had gone through the bushes and tapped at the door.

A small, grey-haired woman opened the door, peered past him at the car, and then looked at him.

"Miss Thatcher?" said Art.

"Arthur," said the small elderly woman. "It must be, I'm sure. Well now."

He was surprised at being Arthur again. For a long time the name had shrunk to Art. He remembered when he had first met Aunt Deborah, how she had not been used to having her name used on her by his mother. He felt as she must have felt, being called Arthur now. He did not use her name at all, but came in as she opened the door for him.

The house had not changed in texture, only in size. And now it had one bedroom and a bathroom, instead of two bedrooms. There was a smell of sour soap in the kitchen.

They had talked, but not very much. Aunt Deborah said she reckoned there wasn't much to tell he'd want to know. How was the guitar? He said the guitar was fine, he had it back at McGuire. He could not tell her that he began the flight to England before the end of the week, because that was information useful to an enemy, though Aunt Deborah was not an enemy, and everyone knew that the B17's at McGuire would fly to Europe in groups.

He had a cup of coffee. Then he left. He said he would write and tell his father how he had found her. She said he should do that; she never got to write to anyone.

He drove on. There was a road, after all, but no one had been this way for some time. He knew that no one lived out on this abandoned beach any more. His grandfather had died seven years before, and the Preacher, five years ago, had gone fishing in his boat and not come back at all.

Now there were three ruins out here. Fire had visited two of them, and the wind the third, laying them all down on their sites so that the sand sifted over the shingles that had been the roofs. There was nothing to tell which house was which. It had not been clear to Arthur, ten or eleven years ago, which house was which as he approached them. Now, to Art, it was no clearer. His grandfather, a man from the alien villages of old England, born nearly a century past in some obscure hamlet, had lived here and left no certain mark. Even his daughter, Aunt Deborah, had not mentioned him this afternoon. Art made a choice about which site was which, and took a little sand from it, and dropped it in a pocket. Then he turned the

151

car, and went back into Arnott's Bay and found the cemetery. He wandered up and down among the stones for some time, until a caretaker told him where to go. Then he found the grave, marked Florence Thatcher, also Benjamin her husband. Below the two names was enough space for Aunt Deborah.

Art drew back a piece of the gritty turf and took a few fingers of gravelly soil from below it. He let that join the sand in his pocket. Now he was set for England. He returned to the car and drove back to McGuire.

Never go back, he thought; and he knew that his second visit had been wasted, and that the sandy gravel in his pocket had been gathered in vain. He would not visit Osney, because that would be a going back as well, and nothing could come from it. The days of his Englishness had stopped in 1886, when his grandfather left England. The B17 was not flying to any place that belonged to him.

But all the same, he wondered afresh when he found, some hours later, that the field they had flown to was three miles from Newmarket, a place his grandfather had worked in, in whose Post Office he had stood. Art wondered, and did not throw the sandy gravel away just yet. But he did not find out where Osney was, either, or which road led to Ely and Wisbech and so to Osney. And there was nothing to remind him, because in this wartime England there were no signposts where roads met, and no place had a name written up.

He went many times to Osney before he knew the name of it. He saw it often from the air. It lay in a corner of the coast, invisible on most days, but on others showing the pale gleam of its church tower from far out to sea. Training flights took the B17's over it at about eight thousand feet, so that if the light was right the tower and the houses could be clearly seen. It was not a name to anyone, or any sort of official landmark.

In the wet of winter water began to lie on the ground, altering the coast without changing its shape. One day there was something that seemed familiar to some part of his memory: there was the sea, close against the land in a high tide, and the land itself was a narrow strip, unmeasurable but distinct, like a floating hair, and there was still water shining behind the filament of shore.

The next day some of the hairline had sunk. Water had joined water and the floods had risen. Rivers that had formerly been helpful in guiding the planes home were now lost, swollen far beyond their banks into meres and new inlets between the higher grounds. A new coast formed itself miles inland. And still there were islands far out, where people waved at the passing bombers; and somewhere in the middle of the sea there still stood the towers of churches.

Osney came to Art one morning. There was no flying that day. He read a local paper that came out once a week. There was nothing else for him to read. A word came up and caught him and then hid itself among the other words. OSNEY, it had said. He searched the page until he found it and then read what was written.

Somebody from the village had been fined at the court in Loddenham for showing a light at night, which was against the law in wartime. The last meeting of the Women's Institute had taken place at Cold Fen Chapel Schoolroom, due to unforeseen circumstances. The prize for Economical Savoury Potato Cakes had been won by Mrs Loving. Art knew that name. Mrs Loving was for him just as much part of the family as all the uncles and aunts who had died in childhood. Their names . . . what were their names? But he read on in the few paragraphs the paper had for Osney.

The Farmers' Union dinner had been presided over by Sir George Ramage, and the chief speaker had been Mr Jack Cartwright, who had talked about the changes in local farming since his aunt, Miss Cartwright of Osney, had been Lord of the Manor and had run the village with a rod of iron and farmed the land as it had been farmed for hundreds of years. Mr Rodney Marks had replied to the speech and said that the coming of the sugar beet crop twenty years ago had had the first big difference since his grandfather had drained Osney Cold Fen seventy years ago. It might be under water now and again, but the crop next year was no worse for it.

To see what he really thought, Art read similar paragraphs about other villages, but they, with strange names, meant nothing to him. The pieces about Osney fitted into his mind as if he belonged to them. He threw the paper down and went to find a map.

Two hours later he was forty-five miles away and drawing a motor cycle to a halt in six inches of water, three hundred yards short of a bridge that stood in the middle of a flood that should have been a banked river. There was no road to be seen going to the bridge, only a tracing of hedges and a dotting of posts to indicate the way. He leaned the motor cycle against a tree and stood beside it on a muddy bank. In a little while a truck came along through the water and stopped when he waved to it. He took a ride on it across the bridge, asking the driver whether he could get through to Osney.

The driver reckoned not, or not from here, not by road at least, though he might walk round on the sea wall if you weren't stopped.

Art got out at the end of the bridge, where the sea-wall started. He had seen it in his mind years before, raised a little above the waters. He had seen it from the air, pencilled faint. Now he found the wall itself narrow, rutted on top with a track, water to the landward side, and mud flats out towards the sea. He went past the sea gates, which were open now to let the water off the land on the dropping tide. Then he was alone between the two seas.

It was a flat, interminable walk. Four miles on, with the mud working its way up between his knees from his ankles, he came in sight of Osney church tower. The countryside was wooded now, with trees up to their branches sometimes in water, so that they were bundles of twigs afloat, no trunks showing, only reflections. Through the trees he could not see how the church stood, whether it was flooded deep as he expected it to be.

Another half mile and he came opposite the village, and could see the houses on the raised ground by the church. There was no way across to them from the sea wall, unless he swam. He was not going to swim, because there was ice hanging in the trees and in the grass of the bank below.

He shouted instead. It was perhaps all he could do, to come as close as he could and then shout. If nothing happened from the shout he would scatter the gravel, still in his pocket, and walk back, his duty done.

The shout was not all that happened. A rowing boat with two men in it came out from the houses and over the water towards him. The men had guns, as well as oars. The guns pointed towards him. But they stopped pointing to him when he waved back and came down the sea wall to meet them, and they saw his uniform. They stared at him rather more than was necessary, he thought, but he found that English people did stare at him in the street. One of the men, though not in uniform, was a police officer, and demanded his papers, first of all. Art was able to satisfy him.

"Thatcher?" said the man, handing the papers back. "That's more like an English name than what we'd, well, expect."

"We thought we might expect someone coming from the sea to be like you, if you see what I mean," said the other man.

"My grandfather," said Art. "He came from Osney."

"Thatcher," said the first man. "Benj Thatcher, that would be. Well, young man, you'd best come back with us and see what there is of the place. 'Tis fairly flooded now, but all the folks be at home, and some would remember." Art got into the boat, and they were rowed over the flood, over hedges and fields and through bushes. "Where first?" said the man.

Art went to the church first. The church was what came to his mind. He knew it was appropriate for a man from the sea, and he recalled now that Parson Ramage kept his dogs in it. He remembered too that the flood of the dream had filled it and he wanted to see whether it had happened.

It had happened. There was a mark on the walls, about a foot up from the ground. The men told him that water had come there this time, and entered the building through the door and it was nearly impossible to dry it out. They went in and found the place a roofed ruin, with silt from the flood staining the ground and lining the wood of the pews, so that it was damp below and white with age and carving above, like an intricate bone in the sand, left by recent tides. In the skin of mud on the floor dogs had run and left the prints of their feet.

"I heard of Parson Ramage," said Art.

"Ah, that was a caution," said one man.

"It was him that started the Methodists at Cold Fen," said the other. "With his wild ways."

They looked next in the churchyard for Martha's grave. They could not get to it because of the water, but they were able to read it. She was one of Art's grandmothers, so he scattered some gravel towards the place. Then they went into the village of Osney itself, and he saw the houses. No one could tell him which one his grandfather had lived in. It was nearly sixty years since he had left, and that was all he could tell them.

He went his own way to Osney Cold Fen, along the raised road that joined the villages. He was hungry now, and not looking forward to his long walk and long ride.

He came to the Chapel first, standing up tall by itself. In its graveyard there was nothing to guide him at all. No stone had a name to it that he knew, except two with Loving on. "Lovink," he said to himself, hoping it was the universal English way to say it.

In the village he found his way at once. One of the houses had a chain fixed to the wall above the door. That, he knew for certain, was the Lovings' house. Opposite there was a small farmhouse with a barn and a garden with fruit trees in it. These two were what he had come to see. He went to the farm house, but there was no one in. He crossed the road, and hoped there was no one in there either. Before he got there he had been seen by children, who gathered more children to themselves, and stared at him. He knew why they stared: they had seen no one like him before. But he was wrong about that, he found in a little while.

He went to the door of the Loving house, and stood by it. He was about to knock, but he heard people inside and waited a moment in case they had seen him and were coming to the door. They did not come. Above him hung the chain, the chain that had bound the man from the sea, that was to hang there until it broke and freed the family of that man.

He put up a hand and lifted the last link from the nail that held it. The weight fell down the steel loops and rested in his hand. He looped some of the flexible heaviness over his wrist and lifted down the centre of the chain, and then the far end, where the iron collar was that had been round the man's neck when he landed.

The chain swung and rapped on the door for him. He gathered it in to himself, understanding every part of it. He remembered things his father had told him, things that his grandfather had perhaps not clearly known. His grandmother, Florence, the mother of his father, had been born a slave, in captivity. In the first years of her life she had known what chains like this, collars like this, were. Art was descended from slaves. The Lovings were descended from a slave. His grandmother had been freed by a war; the man from the sea by escape and shipwreck.

The door of the house opened. A girl held it open. She drew in her breath when she saw him. She was beautiful. But he had not come to find that out, in particular. He had come to see what it was that had formed his grandfather, and to find the graves he loved and lay some earth from his own grave in them, and raise a headstone. He would have to write home for the names of the children.

But now he understood completely why Benjamin Thatcher had married someone born a slave. He saw that this beautiful girl had the same skin as himself, the same skin as his grandmother; that it was part of her beauty. He was himself captured by it too. He tried to put the chain down, but dropped one end of it. Somehow he pulled it in two, and a broken link fell separate to the floor.

It was love at first sight; slow, quiet love. He put up his hand to that dark face, as Benjamin had put his to her grandmother, and she pushed her lips against it, almost in a kiss. Then she kissed it, and the rust from the chain marked her lips and cheek, and his hand, light markings against their dark skins. He had come back to Osney, and now between them they had enough years of freedom to be truly free.